PARA TROUPERS

THE CASE OF **JOHNNY 'THE ROCKET' ESPINOSA**

BOOK 2 OF THE PARA TROUPERS SERIES

I hope you enjoy the book. Take care & be kind.

MARK STEPHEN JOHNSON

Illustrated by Erik Westgard

ISBN: 978-1-6847-1867-2 (sc)
ISBN: 978-1-6847-1866-5 (e)

Illustrated by: Erik Westgard

Lulu Publishing Services rev. date: 02/07/2020

CONTENTS

DEDICATION

Being a high school teacher in the Minneapolis Public Schools, I recognize the daily struggles that some students have with reading. Some have language issues, some find the required reading boring and uninspiring and some just struggle with reading in general. As a result, I wanted to create a book series that students of all reading abilities would find fun and interesting. I have determined that reading of any kind is better than not reading at all. Lifelong reading for enjoyment has been, and will always be, my goal.

I would like to dedicate this book to my students at Washburn High School, and students from around the country, that bring life to the art of teaching. Learning from each other is one of the most rewarding experiences a teacher can have.

I would also like to dedicate this book to my grandchildren, Morgan, Tanner, Madison and Audree. The excitement, love, laughter and sparkle in their eyes cannot help but motivate, and bring life to the books that I write. Morgan has already, at twelve years old, published her first written work, and was recognized by her school for her advanced writing abilities.

Support comes in many forms. The support that I received from our good friends, Jim and Renae Smith, was greatly appreciated. Thanks for being such great friends and curling partners.

I would also like to dedicate this book to Sue. Her consistent encouragement and critiques of this book have enabled me to complete this labor of love and have inspired me to continue realizing my dream of writing. Thank you so much.

In closing, I would also like to acknowledge and thank Erik Westgard for his illustrations in the book and for his cover design. Erik is a student of mine at Washburn High School and has a keen talent and vision for art and design. A bright future lies ahead for Erik.

Chapter 1

A GLORIOUS HISTORY

Juan and I stood at the corner of Espinosa Way and State Highway One reading the wooden sign on the entrance to the old Woodticks Stadium.

"Building Condemned. No Trespassing," I read aloud.

"Sad, isn't it?" responded Juan. "All the history. All the great players that passed through this ball park on their way to the major leagues, and eventually, the Hall of Fame. The gigantic crowds that filled this place gone. And now here it sits, rotting away, the greatest piece of history this town has ever had."

"Yeah, I know. Babe Ruth, Mickey Mantle, Willie Mays, Joe Dimaggio, Harmon Killebrew and our own Johnny 'The Rocket' Espinosa, all laced up their cleats here before making it to the pros," I sighed. "Or maybe I should say, should have made it to the pros."

"Yeah. Poor Johnny," said Juan. "He was only eighteen years old when the Cubs called him up to the major league team. Sadly, he never realized his dream."

"Man, he would've been awesome in the pros!" I concluded. "It's all because of that stupid, drunk, taxi cab driver that crashed his car into that embankment by the stadium. 'The Rocket' didn't even have a chance to show what he could do. They say he died on impact," Juan said.

"Tragic," I agreed. "He was the greatest, hometown player that we ever had here in Spider Lake. 'The Rocket' hit thirty-five home runs in his rookie season with the Woodticks, just out of high school, before being called up to the major league roster. That's damn good for a 'double-A' ball player," I said.

"I know, and talk about speed. He was the fastest player that people had ever seen," Juan blurted out. "Nobody could get around the bases faster than Espinosa. The name 'Rocket' was a perfect description for him."

The city of Spider Lake named the main street in front of the stadium after 'The Rocket' when he passed, to honor his athletic achievements and impact on the city. Eager residents from all over the state would come to watch him play boosting Spider Lake's economy during the baseball season ten-fold, while giving children a real life hero to emulate.

According to all accounts, he was a good young man too, always taking the time to talk to his fans or sign autographs for the youngsters scrambling to get close to him, holding baseballs high into the air, hoping to get noticed. He never disappointed a single one of them. His jerseys were still being worn by kids, to this day, as a testament to his popularity.

About twenty years following the tragedy, the city built a new stadium relegating the old, historic field to its role as an 'eyesore' on the western side of town. In the following thirty years, the older, but more beautiful ballpark, suffered from neglect and vandalism. Almost every inch of its exterior was covered with spray paint, windows had been broken and vandals had taken bricks from the once proud exterior. Even the solid wooden benches from the spectator areas had been stolen. Its rich history was slowly being forgotten.

Juan and I were baseball players and fans. We had played together our whole lives and were deeply saddened that this once great field was going to fall by the wayside and into the annals of history as a footnote in some baseball almanac.

"I wish the Woodticks were still playing here," I said, looking sadly at the old structure in front of me. "I wish we could do something to save this piece of history."

"I do too, but it's not going to happen Marcus," Juan insisted. "The city has that newer, larger..."

"And uglier stadium," I interrupted loudly.

I knew Juan was right. I knew the stadium was not going to be saved. I think that I was more saddened that our yearly ritual of sneaking into the old ballpark, before our baseball season began, was coming to an end.

Each year, in early April, we would sneak into the broken window next to the front gates, crawl through one of the wooden air ducts that supplied fresh air into the locker rooms, and then work our way through the many rows of dilapidated seats and out onto the field. Standing on the pitching mound, we would admire the large spires that protruded upward from the field to the imposing wooden roof that hung over the grandstands. We would sit in the dugouts talking about the great players that sat on that same spot over the decades, while admiring the enormous advertisements painted across the outfield walls from nearly fifty years ago.

We replayed great catches made by the Woodticks outfielders diving into the soft grass of the outfield. We ran the bases pretending that a ball was hit deep into the right field corner. Rounding third base we slid into home plate scoring the winning run to the sound of fake cheering from the massive crowd.

These formative childhood adventures were very important to us. They had become a part of who we were and what we had set for goals in our lives. We were certainly sad to see these traditions end.

We stood across the street for several minutes, just staring at the massive, tired old field, before we headed for home. We glanced back at the stadium every hundred feet or so as we walked, trying to imprint our views of the old field into our memory banks. We didn't want to forget.

We crossed the street, not really paying attention to the cars that were whizzing by. Juan, walking just behind me, leaped onto the curb, shouting obscenities at a car that came perilously close to him as it went speeding by.

The rear window of the car rolled down quickly and two girls from our high school stuck their heads out the window and yelled out to us.

"Hey boys! We love you!" they screamed.

The car's proximity to us startled me. It was a near miss. I wanted to lash out to them in anger for their carelessness, but I recognized one of them as a friend of my sister Courtney.

Not wanting to make a scene, I only mustered a feeble wave in response.

"Damn. That was close," Juan said, slightly shaken from the incident. "I think my life passed before my eyes."

We were used to a lot of attention since last summer's adventure at the Old Rutledge mansion. That investigation had made us local celebrities. Strangers from all over Spider Lake had been reaching out to us wanting to hear the stories about our adventure, or to share their own paranormal experiences with us, ever since we rid the town of the evil that the mansion possessed.

Being recognized as a celebrity was not something that we had planned on when we formed our Para Troupers group last year, designed to rid Spider Lake of all evil entities.

The Rutledge case became the talk of the town, a wake-up call to residents to 'come to grips with the reality' that ghosts exist. Discussions about the paranormal became common fodder from barber shops to gas stations and shoe stores. Talk about ghosts had become so popular, that our fledgling group of paranormal investigators had become the place where residents went to when they had an issue with a ghost.

We continued our walk along Highway One, which was pretty quiet at this time of the evening, long after the end of the work day and whatever rush hour traffic this tiny town could muster.

"Hey man," said Juan.

"Yeah?" I asked.

"Hearing the crowd cheering is something that I never get tired of," Juan said, as his longer, dark hair blew into his face from the strong wind at our backs. "You know, I can't believe that we can hear the crowd in the new stadium from here. It must be a mile away."

"Oh yeah," I agreed, stopping for a moment while straining to hear the sounds. "The wind must be carrying the voices in our direction."

"Yeah, weird," Juan laughed.

We continued down the sidewalk for fifty feet or so until Juan stopped, glanced back at the old stadium, and then looked at me.

"What's up?" I asked Juan.

"Marcus, the new stadium is that way, right?" asked Juan, pointing directly in front of us.

"Yeah, so?" I asked.

"The wind is at our backs. How can we possibly hear the sounds from the new ballpark when its in front of us?" he questioned.

"Damn, you're right Juan!" I blurted out while turning into the wind behind us. "Where are the voices coming from then?"

We both stood on the sidewalk, looking at the old Woodtick Stadium, about two blocks behind us. We stood there quietly trying to catch more voices in the wind.

"No way," Juan laughed loudly.

"Not possible," I said.

"Is it possible?" Juan started.

"No! No way!" I interrupted. "They can't be coming from the old stadium."

As we stood there on the sidewalk, we caught more voices in the wind.

Batting first.... (Unintelligible wind noises).... Number one.... (unintelligible).... The... (unintelligible) Espinosa!

The sound of the voice was slightly drowned out by the wind blowing through our ears. We stood there, motionless, listening for more. My back was feeling tingly. I felt light-headed. Juan's mouth was open wide, his eyes as large as saucers.

I managed to blurt out a few words.

"It's coming from there!" I said, pointing to the old stadium.

"It sounds like the old Woodtick public address announcer," Juan said. "You know, the one that announced the Woodtick games fifty years ago!"

"The one from the YouTube videos?" I asked. "What the....?"

"I don't know man," Juan interrupted, kicking a few rocks off the sidewalk. "I am freaked out."

"It sounded like the announcer was introducing Johnny 'The Rocket' Espinosa as the next hitter," I said.

"Yeah. I know," said Juan, with both hands clasping the sides of his head.

We stood there for a few more minutes, trying to hear anything else that was being carried on the wind, but nothing was heard.

"Man, I am freaked out!" Juan yelled. "That was AWESOME!" he continued.

I couldn't help but laugh at Juan's reaction. We had never experienced anything like that before.

"Juan?" I asked

"Yeah Marcus?" he responded.

"That is the very definition of a residual haunting. When ghostly noises are heard from the past, and they repeat themselves over and over again, like a recording, ingrained in the fabric of time. It doesn't seem like an intelligent haunt to me, you know, where the entity interacts with you," I explained.

"Well, whatever that was, I want to hear it again," Juan joked.

"Me too," I laughed.

Our conversation had quickly changed from reminiscing about the old ballpark, to the reality and excitement, of what we just experienced.

"Do you really think the stadium is haunted Marcus?" Juan timidly asked.

"Well, how else do you explain what we heard?" I asked.

Juan's mood suddenly soured.

"What's wrong man?" I asked.

"Well, I'm even more bummed out now," said Juan, his face looking down to the ground. "The stadium will be gone soon. They're putting up that new apartment complex on the site. Can you believe it?"

"I feel the same way," I agreed, looking back at the magnificent structure fading into the distance as we shuffled ahead. "Why does Spider Lake always tear down cool, old stuff and put up new, ugly crap in the name of progress?"

"I don't get it," Juan agreed, shaking his head.

"Hey! You know what we should do?" I said. "We should bring our ghost hunting gear and explore the sounds of the ballpark. Maybe we could capture what we just heard. How cool would that be?"

"That's not a bad idea," Juan rationalized. "Do you think the girls would want to come with?"

"Damn straight they would", I agreed. "This is right in the Para Trouper's wheelhouse. I'll send Veronica a message later and get back to ya. "

"Awesomeness!" Juan yelled out. "We're back!"

We parted ways and went home. My heart was racing with excitement.

Holy crap, I thought. *This might not rise to the level of a life or death investigation like the Rutledge case did, but we might be able to document some of the sounds we heard at the ballpark. We haven't worked with a residual haunt yet. This could open up new investigations for us.*

I raced home and flung open the back door that led into the kitchen. I ran into the house knocking a bottle of ketchup onto the floor with my backpack that was over my right shoulder. I hadn't been this excited, or motivated, since the Rutledge case.

"Whoa, whoa there Marcus!" my mom shouted. "What gives? Your lucky that ketchup hadn't been opened yet. That would've been a big mess for you to clean up. How many times do I have to tell you that you need to slow down when you're in the house?"

My heart was racing and my breathing was rapid. My eyes were bulging with excitement.

"It looks like you, well..., saw a ghost!" my mom laughed as she sat at the kitchen table.

"You could say that," I responded, slightly out of breath. "I'll tell you about it later."

I ran into the living room and up the stairs to my bedroom leaving my mom speechless, and very curious, I'm sure. I needed to call Veronica and get her up to speed. Veronica and Dez were the other half of our paranormal investigative team.

Veronica and I liked each other as friends, but we were slowly become more than that. She was very smart, undeniably pretty, very edgy and she played the guitar, making her the coolest person I've ever known.

Dez was cute, a perfectionist, a brilliant student and very goal oriented. She was the most cautious of the group, rarely taking chances, but not afraid to stand up to anyone, or anything.

We made quite the team. Driven by our love of the paranormal and our desire to rid Spider Lake of evil entities, our foursome was ready to tackle even the most difficult cases.

I threw my backpack on the bed and quickly dialed Veronica.

"Hey Marcus," she answered. "How are you today?"

"Great Veronica," I responded. "I haven't seen you in a couple of weeks. How was the big, family camping trip?"

"Oh, you know," Veronica stated. "It was alright. Mount Rushmore was still there like the last time we went a few years ago."

I laughed. I really missed her when she was gone.

"Yeah. It was pretty quiet here," I said, surprisingly nervous while attempting to make small talk with her. "Hey, Juan and I were just walking by the old ballpark on Espinosa Way, you know, the old Woodticks Stadium."

"Oh, I love that old thing. Too bad it was condemned last year," Veronica responded.

"Yeah, about that," I said. "We were walking by the old place earlier and heard some crazy sounds, you know, voices from the ballpark."

"Really?" she asked. "What kind of voices?"

"Like the public address announcer, the crowd cheering, just voices," I responded.

"Wow. Cool," Veronica gasped. "What were you guys doing over there anyway?"

"We sneak in every year to just walk on the same field as all those great players of the past," I said.

"Wow. Cool. Do you think the place is haunted?" she asked.

"We do, but we think that it's more of a residual haunt, not intelligent," I explained.

"Are you thinking that we should investigate it?" Veronica asked, clearly excited.

"Yeah, we do. Interested?" I questioned.

"Hell yeah," she responded in typical Veronica fashion. "This would give us a new perspective on this type of haunt," she said.

"Hey can you call Dez for me and let her know about this?" I asked. "I don't think she'd want to miss this either. Message me later. I'll be up late, as usual."

"You got it Marcus!" she answered. "Talk to ya later."

It had been a while since our Para Troupers group had a good investigation. Since the Rutledge case, only several other real opportunities presented themselves to us. We solved all of the cases.

One of them ended up being a hoax. Some seniors at our high school sent us to a vacant home, set up some fake ghostly stuff and tried to scare us.

Another investigation ended up being a case of mistaken identity when a large racoon had entered an abandoned home. A neighbor heard noise coming from the old place and called us after police had found nothing unusual.

After a few of these types of cases, we were ready for a real ghostly investigation.

I was eager to get to bed, so when eleven o'clock came around, I was ready. I went to say goodnight to my parents who were watching the Late Show on the living room television. I stood at the bottom of the stairs, trying not to seem too happy about getting to bed.

"Marcus...you're ready for bed already?" my mom chuckled.

"We usually have to tell you five thousand times to go to bed every night," my dad said, seemingly annoyed.

"Yeah, well you know. It's going to be a long day tomorrow at school," I stammered, trying to make it sound like it wasn't a big deal.

"Alright then Honey. Good night," my mom said with her typical warm smile.

"Good night son," my dad said.

"Good night," I responded before running up the stairs to group text with my friends.

"What the Hell was that all about?" my dad questioned.

"I'm not sure Dear," my mom answered. "But knowing Marcus, it's probably not good."

Chapter 2

VOICES IN THE NIGHT

I stayed up past midnight texting with our Para Trouper team about the old Woodticks Stadium, deciding what paranormal detection devices we would need and picking a day for our investigation. We were all upbeat and positive. We were definitely prepared with all of the paranormal equipment that we possessed, and we were hungry and excited for some real investigating.

When we finally ended our furious texting session, I was pretty tired and ready to sleep. I plugged in my phone and was sound asleep in just a few minutes.

I very rarely woke up during the night, for any reason. My family often joked about my sleeping habits, saying that they would have to drag me out of the house, while still sleeping, if it was on fire.

I also had an uncanny knack for remembering my dreams each morning. As a matter of fact, I looked forward to going to bed because most of my dreams were so intense, I couldn't wait to see what I was in store for each night.

One night I might be hitting a home run, helping the Woodticks win another championship. The next night I might be eating dinner with Cody "The Hammer" Johnson, discussing how he single-handedly beat the Yankees to win the American League pennant. Or how he drove a line drive so hard into the stands, it smashed into the head of a poor woman looking the other way, killing her instantly, while splattering blood three rows deep into the stands.

As one could tell, most of my dreams centered around baseball my whole life, up until recently that is. Dreams of Veronica had taken over my inner thoughts, and tonight would be no different.

I was deep into a Veronica dream. We were sitting on a dock by the Spider Lake shore under a row of maple trees, dipping our bare feet into the cold water. There was barely a wisp of wind, leaving the water's surface as shiny and clear as glass.

Veronica leaned in for a passionate kiss. I responded quickly, beginning a long, steamy make-out session.

As we kissed, a deep, baritone voice loudly interrupted our scene. Startled, we stopped and looked up, thinking that someone was physically next to us putting a stop to our fun.

The man spoke again, this time a little softer. I began to slowly awaken into that 'in-between' zone, halfway between a dream state and reality.

I slowly opened one eye, thinking that if I only opened up one, I wouldn't wake up too much. My eye scanned the entire room. No one was there! Figuring that the voice was part of the dream, I closed my eye and desperately tried to return to my dream with Veronica. My efforts were to no avail. This persistent voice clearly wanted to get my attention.

"*Marcus... Marcus,*" I heard.

I must be dreaming, I thought, rolling onto my left side. But the voice continued.

"*Marcus! You've gotta stop it from happening! Help them.*"

I was half-dazed, but I clearly heard that male voice. I laid there in bed. My alarm hadn't gone off yet. I looked over at the clock.

"*Marcus! Stop them!*" the voice said with urgency.

Alright. I clearly heard that, I thought.

I rolled onto my other side wondering who I was listening to. Chills rolled up and down my spine as I could feel a presence in the room with me. I looked over at the clock again. I began to sweat.

Oh My God! I thought. *It was only three o'clock in the morning! How was I supposed to get to sleep now?*

I rolled over onto my pillow, still half-dazed. I thought that God was punishing me for staying up late talking with friends instead of sleeping.

I laid there waiting for another message for what seemed like hours, but nothing happened. There were no new messages. I struggled to relax. I was so exhausted.

Then I heard a clicking noise, and then music. My alarm was going off!

This can't be, I thought.

I rolled over to shut it off, mumbling obscenities out loud.

"Man this sucks," I said quietly.

I slowly sat up in bed with my feet firmly planted on the ground.

This is going to be a long day, I said to myself. *And what the heck was that voice telling me? They need help? Stop them? What does that even mean? Ugh.*

I stumbled to the bathroom and proceeded to get ready for school. I shaved all four whiskers on my chin, got dressed and headed downstairs. Not feeling hungry in the least, I skipped breakfast and headed off to the bus stop with my backpack draped over my shoulder. I needed to be there just before seven in the morning to catch the bus. Much to my surprise, I was almost five minutes early.

I stood next to a few annoying middle schoolers, talking so loudly, they could have woken the dead in the next county. I cleared my throat to get their attention, and then stared them down with a "stinky eye" that immediately shut them up.

Juan slowly approached the bus stop. He was very quiet and yawning incessantly. His normal upbeat attitude picked me up most mornings. It was unusual to see him this way. He looked like he hadn't slept in months.

"Sup man?" I questioned.

"Man, I did not sleep well last night," Juan explained. "I kept waking up all night long. It may sound stupid, but I thought that someone was talking to me."

"It must have been a bad dream Juan," I chuckled.

"It wasn't a dream, the voice was whispering in my ears," he shot back. "I clearly heard it."

I glared back at Juan, my cloggy, morning head was suddenly as clear as a crisp winter evening.

"Voices? What did the voices say to you?" I asked impatiently, as the bus pulled up to the corner.

"Let's get to our seats. I'll tell you then," Juan mumbled.

We sat in our assigned seats. I immediately looked at Juan to continue our conversation. He just sat there, put his head back and then started to fall asleep.

"Juan!" I said, while grabbing his coat sleeve and shaking it until his eyes opened. "What did the voice say to you last night?"

"Oh yeah," Juan said. "Sorry. I'm just so tired. Umm...they kept telling me that I needed to stop it from happening, and I needed to help them."

I was stupefied, unable to speak. I felt as if my eyes were open so far that my eyeballs may just fall out onto the bus floor. I could only muster three words.

"What the Hell?" I said loudly.

"Quiet man!" Juan whispered loudly. "Talking like that will get us in trouble with the bus driver."

"Hey. I don't care," I said, grabbing Juan's coat with both hands and pulling his face closer to mine. "I got the same messages last night, around three o'clock!"

"What?" Juan asked. "How is that possible?"

I sat back in my seat facing the front of the bus, stunned. Juan did the same. It took a minute to process our conversation before I could spit out an explanation.

"They say that three o'clock is the bewitching hour, the time that most ghostly entities are active," I explained. "Maybe this ghost wants to get a message to us."

"But help them? Who are they?" Juan asked. "What are we supposed to be stopping? And why us?"

"I don't know yet," I answered. "But we need to find out. Do we know anyone that has died recently Juan?"

"Damn, not that I know of," Juan whispered. "Oh wait, my uncle Leo died last year!"

"Did you know him well?" I asked.

"No. He lived in New York. I haven't seen him in years," Juan explained.

"Hmmm, I don't think that'd be him," I said. "He lived too far away and you didn't even know him. He has no reason to come to us."

The rear wheel on the bus ran up onto the curb as it was rounding a corner, practically throwing me into the aisle.

"Sorry kids!" yelled out Johnny, our bus driver. "Didn't see that one coming."

He laughed, looking directly into the rear view mirror at me, as the bus continued to barrel down the street.

"That's okay Johnny," Juan called out. "We needed to wake up any way."

Johnny laughed, while keeping eye contact with me.

I put my hand over my mouth. My eyes opened widely.

"Juan! That's it!" I said loudly.

"I know Marcus. But I was kidding. I didn't want to be woken up that way," Juan explained.

"No, no! What if it was Johnny that came to us in our dreams last night?" I asked.

Johnny, the bus driver, smiled at my question.

"Why would a bus driver come to us in our dreams Marcus?" Juan laughed. "Does he want driving tips from us?"

"No, no Juan," I said. "What if it was Johnny 'The Rocket' Espinosa that had come to us in our dreams?"

"Now THAT would make sense," Juan said. "But, how do you figure?"

"Well, we both heard noises coming from the ballpark yesterday right?" I asked.

Juan nodded.

"The public address announcer was announcing 'The Rocket' as the next hitter, right?" I asked.

Juan agreed.

"Well, it just seems pretty coincidental that both things happen on the same day, doesn't it?" I surmised.

"It does," Juan said, while scratching his head. "But, why would 'The Rocket' ask us to help them, and then tell us to stop it from happening? It makes no sense."

"Stop it from happening may mean the tearing down of the Woodtick Stadium?" I questioned.

"Hmmm. Maybe." Juan answered. "But help who? The ghosts of players, now deceased, stuck in the stadium?"

"Maybe," I responded. "Maybe anyone that went to the games, the umpires, the announcers? I don't know. I wonder how many people have died at the old Woodtick Stadium over the years. We need to do a little research before we start investigating the stadium."

"Yeah, for sure Marcus," Juan blurted out as the bus pulled up to the school and the door swung open.

"See ya kids," Johnny the bus driver said as he watched us exit the bus.

We walked down the stairs and stood on the sidewalk as we repositioned our backpacks over our shoulders.

"Hey boys!" Johnny the bus driver called out to us. "I think you're on the right track. They need help, and fast."

The bus door closed and Johnny sped away. I looked over at Juan, who was already staring at me.

"What did he say?" I asked.

"Yeah, you heard right Marcus," Juan said. "I heard it too."

"What the Hell?" I blurted out. "Does Johnny know about our plan? Did he overhear us? What does he know about our dreams and the sounds from the ballpark?"

"Maybe Johnny the bus driver is really Johnny 'The Rocket' Espinosa and he faked his death years ago!" Juan proclaimed.

"That's an interesting theory Juan, but 'The Rockets' body was found at the crash sight, and his family had an open casket funeral. Everyone saw him dead," I said.

"I don't know Marcus, why would Johnny the bus driver say what he did if he didn't have information that could help us out?" Juan said.

We were quite confused as we headed into the school and to our lockers, just a few feet apart from each other. Our conversation continued until a familiar voice called out breaking our intense discussion.

"Hey boys!"

It was Dez, approaching us with her hands full of books for class.

"Hey Dezzy," I yelled out. "Did Veronica talk to you about the stadium?"

"I sure did," a voice from behind me stated.

I'd recognize that voice anywhere. It was Veronica.

"Hi Juan," she smiled. "And hi to you Marcus," she said as she rubbed her shoulder in to mine.

My face was as red as a ripened tomato from my Grandma Abby's house.

"Hi girls!" Juan said.

"Hi Veronica," I said confidently.

Juan couldn't hold back and abruptly blurted out what we experienced with Johnny the bus driver.

"Johnny the bus driver, we think, is Johnny 'The Rocket' Espinosa," he blurted out. "We think he knows about the ghostly sounds coming from the stadium and about our dreams from last night."

"Well, that's not exactly true Juan," I interrupted. "We don't know anything for sure yet! Johnny is probably just a bus driver and we have no proof that he knows anything about the stadium voices we heard, or our dreams."

"Geez, you guys, you need to fill us in on the details! What exactly is going on? And what dreams did you have last night?" Dez asked.

"Yeah, why don't you just ask Johnny the bus driver what he knows. You see him every day, right?" Veronica asked. "Ask him what his last name is. Ask him what he knows about the old Woodticks Stadium, and then ask him if he ever played baseball!"

"Great idea Veronica!" Juan said. "What's the worst thing that could happen?"

"Exactly!" Veronica said.

"Well, he might get ticked off and refuse to drive you guys anymore," Dez surmised.

"Nah. He's not the type to get mad at all," I said. "We'll do it!"

"You know, Veronica and I don't take the bus anymore," Dez said. "So you guys can talk with Johnny, and Veronica and I will round up all the ghost hunting equipment after school today."

"When do you guys want to gather evidence at the stadium?" Veronica asked.

"Let's do Friday night, after dinner," I said. "I think we should bring all of our equipment from Mrs. Ardene Miller too."

Mrs. Miller was a long time local paranormal expert, now retired, that gave us the much-needed equipment.

"We should consult with her as well. Her expertise on the Rutledge case was so incredibly helpful," Juan said.

"Juan and I also think that we should do some research about the stadium to see if there were any deaths recorded at the location," I said. "Or any other reason why we are hearing the ghostly voices from the past."

"Great idea Marcus," Veronica agreed. "Why don't we do that this evening? We still have a couple of days until our Friday investigation."

"After we complete our tasks, let's meet at my place, at say, seven o'clock?" Dez asked.

"Let's do this." I said. "If we find out anything from Johnny, I will let you know tonight."

"Great. See you later you guys!" said Dez.

"Hold on here. We still need to hear about these dreams from last night," Veronica blurted out. "What do your dreams have to do with this investigation?"

"Well," I started, "Juan and I had the exact same dream last night. At least I think it was a dream. Someone was talking to us, telling us to 'stop it from happening' and 'do it for them', or something like that."

"Wow, freaky!" Dez said.

"I know," explained Juan. "Help who, and stop what from happening?"

"Cool!," said Veronica. "This is going to be frickin awesome."

"Tell me about it," I responded. "Let's get this research done though tonight. It may be eye-opening."

The girls parted ways and started off to class.

"Call me later Marcus!" said Veronica, smiling at my red face and walking away.

"Yup, I will." I responded.

"Boy, you got it bad for her, don't you Marcus?" said Juan.

"What are you talkin about Juan?" I responded.

Juan gently shoved me and smiled as he slammed his locker door shut.

"What? Am I giving off some pretty obvious signals to everyone?" I asked.

"What do you think Marcus?" Juan laughed as he made his way through the crowd in the hallway.

I stood there for a moment, adjusting my books in my hands, and went off to class.

School days always seemed so long to me. I knew that school was something I had to do, a required part of childhood. But what I really wanted to do was to skip over the school part and proceed directly to adulthood, where my life could be fun. I looked forward to the evenings, and especially, the weekends without school.

Adults have it easy, I always thought. *All they have to do is go to work and make money.*

The drudgery of school ended with the three o'clock bell. I raced to my locker and found Juan waiting with eager anticipation.

"C'mon man. Let's talk to Johnny the bus driver," Juan said, rushing me along. "I have some burning questions for him."

We raced out to the bus area and climbed on board our bus, number forty-four. Much to our surprise, Johnny wasn't there.

"Hey, where's Johnny?" I asked the bus driver. "He's always here, every day."

"Honey," the woman bus driver said. "I've been driving this bus number forty-four for seventeen years now. There ain't no such person as Johnny. As a matter of fact, there ain't no Johnny anywhere in our town's fleet of bus drivers."

"That's impossible, ma'am," I said. "We've been talking to Johnny every day, on this bus, since school started this fall."

"Ha ha! I ain't never heard that one before," she laughed.

Juan reached out to a middle schooler seated by the front door of the bus.

"Hey, kid, who has been our bus driver all year?" Juan asked.

The kid took a second to respond and then finally answered.

"Ms. Bella."

Totally embarrassed, and surprised by his unexpected answer, I grabbed Juan's coat and pulled him to our seat.

"What the Hell is going on Juan?" I pleaded.

"I haven't got a clue," he responded. "We see Johnny everyday, and now apparently he never existed? Are we losing it Marcus?"

"Wow. Just wow!" I answered.

The hair on the back of my neck stood on end. I was caught by surprise.

"We need to think this through Juan. What just happened here?" I asked quietly.

"What if Johnny truly never existed?" I asked. "What if we are seeing things now? What if we're losing it Juan?"

"How could Johnny not exist?" Juan asked. "How could Johnny take over Ms. Bella's body, every day on the bus, and we are the only ones that notice? I don't know about you Marcus, but I feel sick to my stomach."

"Me too Juan," I said, holding my stomach. "Me too."

Chapter 3

HELP FROM BEYOND

Juan and I got off the bus at our stop, took a few steps over to Mrs. Fraction's yard, and then sat down on the soft grass to continue our conversation.

"That's crazy isn't Juan?" I asked.

"You've got that right Marcus, my man," Juan responded.

"We need to go to the library, like today," I said. "Like now. We need answers to a lot of questions."

Juan stood up, adjusting his backpack.

"Um, let me drop my stuff off and check in with my mom. I'll be over to pick you up in about 10 minutes," Juan said.

"Great," I agreed.

We both took off running in opposite directions. We lived about a half a block away from each other, on the same street.

I ran in through the back door throwing my backpack onto the floor in the dining room.

"Marcus!" said my dad sternly.

I turned to see him chopping some vegetables for dinner through the kitchen doorway.

"Yeah Dad?" I responded innocently.

"C'mon Marcus, is that where your backpack goes? And why are you always running? You should take some of that energy you have and put it to good use around here," he suggested.

"Sorry Dad," I responded, grabbing my backpack. "Juan and I are heading to the library to do some research for a project. We'll be back in a couple of hours at the most."

"Really? You never cease to amaze me Marcus," my dad said. "I bet you haven't stepped into that library since you were in the sixth grade."

"Yeah, I know," I shot back. "This is really an important assignment. I want to get on it right away."

"Alright," he said, nodding his approval. "Be back by six o'clock though. I'm making my chicken stir fry that everyone likes. Don't be late!"

"I won't Dad," I said.

I ran upstairs and threw my backpack in my bedroom, then raced downstairs to answer the front doorbell.

"I got it Dad!" I yelled. "It's Juan! I can't believe he got here already!"

I opened the door only to see the Fedex driver standing on the front porch.

"Oh hi...um...can I help you?" I asked.

The driver was tall and thin, his uniform pressed to perfection. The driver had a nametag on his front left shirt pocket that read 'Johnny'. I just stared at it for a couple of seconds.

"C'mon kid, whatcha lookin at? Sign here," was all the driver would say.

I signed my name. He handed me a single plain envelope with my first name written on the front of it. No return address or postage was stamped on it anywhere. The driver ran back to his truck and took off in a hurry. I stood there on the porch looking at the envelope in my hand.

I opened the envelope and pulled out a single notecard with some words on it. I read it aloud.

"**Release them from their pain. They need help**," I read.

Juan ran up the front sidewalk just in time to see my jaw hanging open staring at the notecard.

"Are you okay Marcus?" he asked.

"Uh. I don't know," was all I could come up with.

I handed the notecard to Juan to read.

"**Release them from their pain. They need help**," Juan read aloud. "Where did you get this from Marcus?"

"Believe it or not, from the Fedex driver," I said. "By the way, his name was Johnny!"

"What? That is quite a coincidence," Juan explained. "Here, let's check the slip you signed. They always write the drivers name on it."

"Here it is right here," Juan said pointing to the line that says 'drivers name'.

"It says Jackson," I said. "But that's impossible. His nametag said Johnny."

"Wow. Weird," said Juan. "It's just like Johnny the bus driver. We are seeing the name Johnny in places where there is no Johnny."

"Obviously, this Johnny is trying to get a very important message to us," I said. "It must be Johnny 'The Rocket' that's trying to connect with us. It's the only Johnny we know of."

"C'mon, let's get to the library," Juan said pulling at my arm.

"Yeah, yeah," I said. "Let's go!"

We left right away and arrived in just a few short minutes at the main entrance of the Spider Lake library.

We approached the main desk and immediately noticed the man working behind the counter checking out books.

"Marcus...look at his nametag!" Juan whispered loudly while nudging his elbow into my side.

"Holy crap!" I whispered back at Juan. "It says Johnny!"

We waited in line for a minute or two contriving a plan to talk with this man.

"What should we say?" Juan asked.

"Um... maybe we could explain what we are looking for and he could point us in the right direction?" I answered.

The man (Johnny) was a very tall man of African-American decent. He was wearing a red and gray sweater vest.

We approached slowly until the man made eye contact.

"How can I help you boys?" Johnny the librarian asked.

He was a very tall, imposing man and had a very deep voice.

"Well sir, we are looking for information on the old Woodtick baseball stadium," I nervously answered.

Johnny smiled.

"You play baseball, do ya boys?" he asked.

"We do sir," Juan responded.

We had no idea what to ask him. Johnny thought for a moment and then asked another question.

"Are you looking for players histories? For information about the teams that came here to play? About the stadium itself? What exactly are you looking for?" he asked.

"Well sir, we are looking for any information on the people that worked there, fans that attended games, managers, owners, players, anyone that that may have died or been killed there, you know, that kind of stuff," Juan answered.

"Well now, that's interesting," Johnny the librarian, said, chuckling at Juan's answer.

"I think you may find everything you need to know back in our microfiche area. We have readers that you look into. You'll find every newspaper article ever written in Spider Lake."

"Wow, thanks sir," I said.

"Sure. You may want to concentrate on the years 1931 and 1932 in particular," Johnny the librarian said.

"Why's that sir?" Juan asked.

"If you want to help them, all you need to know will be in those two years," Johnny said.

Juan and I just looked at each other.

"Thank you sir," I said.

"Good luck with your search, boys," he said. "But remember, if this isn't done quickly, souls may be lost forever."

We turned and looked at each other for a split second before I turned back to thank him.

"Thanks Johnny..." I started.

"He's gone!" Juan said loudly.

"You'll have to be quiet in here you two," the woman behind the desk, answered. "If you can't be quiet, you'll have to leave."

"I'm sorry ma'am," I responded.

We started to walk to the microfiche area in the back of the library.

"Wow, can you believe that Marcus?" Juan blurted out. "That's the third Johnny we've encountered today that had a message for us!"

"I know. This is so weird," I answered. "We have never encountered anything like this before. But, I think that we're on the right track. Let's see what we can find on the microfiche readers."

"Here Marcus. You take that one. I'll take this one," Juan said.

"I'll do 1931 and you do 1932, okay Juan?" I asked.

"No prob Marcus. We've got this!" Juan shot back.

"We need to take our time so we don't miss anything!" I added. "Look for anything that may have produced a ghost."

We worked on the microfiche for about an hour before Juan made a discovery.

"Hey Marcus?" Juan asked.

"Did you find something Juan?" I responded.

"Yeah. On June 3rd, 1932, a fan died of heart failure while eating a hot dog behind the third base dugout," Juan explained.

"What was his name?" I asked.

"Um... Kenny Krumpis it says," Juan read.

"Okay, write it down Juan," I directed.

A few minutes passed before I found one as well.

"Hey Juan. I've got one too," I said.

"On May 14th, 1931, a Spider Lake woman, Jennifer Stone, was killed when a line drive, off the bat of Cody 'The Hammer' Johnson, struck her in the side of the head, killing her instantly."

"Wow. Tragic!" Juan said.

I sat there quietly, slumping in my chair.

"Marcus, you okay?" Juan asked.

"Oh my God Juan!" I said quietly. "This incident has been in my dreams before."

"What?" Juan gasped.

"Yeah, the whole Jennifer Stone thing. I've had that whole tragedy play out in my dreams multiple times as I sat with Cody 'The Hammer' Johnson, having dinner."

"Really? Wow, man. Awesome!" Juan said.

I know," I explained. "I can see it now. Apparently she was talking with the woman next to her and didn't see the hard hit line drive coming. They had to call the game so they could clean up all the blood that had splattered all over."

"Oh, that must've been an ugly scene," Juan said.

"Apparently, Cody 'The Hammer' Johnson was so distraught at what happened, he was never the same ballplayer again. By the end of the season, his promising career was over," I explained.

"You better write that one down too Marcus!," Juan said. "It must be related to Johnny somehow."

We stayed for over two hours looking for any deaths that happened near or in the stadium in that two-year span. We found a total of six deaths in 1931 and four deaths in 1932. In addition to the tragic Ms. Stone case, there were six heart related deaths and one double murder-suicide.

We learned that the murder involved a married woman who was at the game with her secret boyfriend on July 17th, 1932. When the woman's husband found out about her affair, he came to the stadium and confronted the pair with a handgun. He killed his wife and her lover and then killed himself in the concession stand area, behind the third base dugout, after cops had given chase and were closing in.

There was so much blood at the scene, the Woodtick organization decided to remove all the concrete and blood-splattered walls in that area after washing it failed to properly clean up the mess. Fresh concrete and brick were installed, removing all evidence of the slaying from the stadium.

"So, it appears that the only violent deaths that occurred during those two years was a result of the double murder-suicide," Juan surmised. "The voices that we are hearing, and the multiple Johnny sightings, must be referring to them."

"And 'The Rocket' knows that those poor people's spirits must be stuck at the stadium. He must want us to help their spirits move on before the stadium's demolition," I stated confidently.

"Yeah, maybe" Juan said. "Let's see if any of this information will help us out on Friday night when we investigate. If it doesn't help us, or we determine that it's not this poor murdered couple, I'm not sure what we'll do next."

We packed up our stuff and headed for home, concluding that we had thoroughly researched those two years at the stadium, and had a couple of good leads.

Juan's phone began to buzz. He reached into his front pocket and looked at the screen.

"Oh, it's Dezzy," Juan said.

"Hi Dez. Whattup?" Juan asked.

"You did?" Juan said. "Awesome. And do we have some crazy news for you two as well."

Juan put his hand over his phone and looked at me.

"Hey Marcus. The girls got all the equipment together and dozens of back up batteries. They're bringing the stuff to our meeting tonight at seven," Juan explained. "We can tell them all about our multiple Johnny sightings."

"Yeah. Sounds great!" I said.

"Okay Dezzy. See you then," Juan said, before hanging up the phone.

"Great. It's all coming together, isn't Juan?" I asked.

"We are back baby!!" Juan yelled out as we fist bumped.

Juan and I high-tailed it back home for supper. I made it back at six o'clock like I had promised my dad earlier. The family was just sitting down at the dinner table as I walked in the front door.

"You made it," my dad proudly stated. "I wasn't sure if you'd get here on time or not."

"Of course Dad," I confidently said. "I'm a man of my word."

My sister, Courtney, laughed aloud as I sat next to her at the table.

"Courtney, it's not nice to laugh at people," my mom explained.

"It just sounded funny. Marcus isn't a man yet," Courtney chuckled.

"Oh, I suppose when I saved your ass at the Rutledge place last year, I wasn't acting manly?" I blurted out.

"C'mon kids, no fighting, or swearing, at the dinner table," my dad said, looking directly at me.

Courtney was a good sister, but her big mouth had always caused many fights between us. I had developed a short fuse when it came to her.

"Sorry Dad," I said. "Is it okay if I go over to Dezzy's tonight at seven o'clock? We are discussing a possible case."

"Sure Honey," my mom answered. "What case are you working on?"

"Um, we are hearing voices, and sounds, from the old Woodticks Stadium and we want to find out what they're trying to tell us," I said to the family.

"Cool," my dad responded. "I don't think you're allowed to be in there though. Aren't there no trespassing signs posted?"

"There is, but it's safe," I explained. "Juan and I, and many others, have been in there walking around the field just looking at it. It's no big deal."

"No trespassing means no trespassing," my dad said.

"Honey, I've got a possible answer for that," my mom said. "The company I work for is doing the demolition of the stadium. I can ask them for permission for your group."

"Awesome Mom!" I said loudly.

"I'll do that tomorrow and text you their answer," she said.

"Thanks Mom. I'm tired of sneaking around all the time. We want to be above board when investigating paranormal stuff," I said.

"You're welcome Marcus," she responded.

I helped clean up after dinner and went upstairs to get ready for the evening. It felt good to be upfront and honest about our plans. I just hoped that my mom's company gave us permission to investigate. If they didn't pull through for us, you can bet that we'll still investigate with or without approval.

Chapter 4

A MYSTERIOUS TURN

Veronica and Juan decided to pick me up before heading over to Dezzy's house for our seven o'clock meeting. Veronica was the first to arrive at my house, ringing the doorbell. My mom was there to warmly greet her at the door.

"Good evening Veronica," my mom said.

"Good evening Mrs. Miller," Veronica responded, giving my mom a big hug.

Veronica was well-liked by my parents. They were genuinely happy to see each other.

"Hi Mr. Miller," Veronica yelled out to my dad watching television in the living room.

My dad came into the foyer area and hugged Veronica.

"Good evening young lady," he said to her. "How have you been Veronica?"

"Oh great!" she answered.

"Marcus told us a little about your next investigation. It sounds quite interesting, me being a baseball fan and all," my dad said.

"Yeah Veronica," I interrupted. "My mom is going to try and get special permission for us to do an investigation at the old Woodticks Stadium."

"Awesome, Mrs. M," Veronica said loudly, looking at my mom.

"We'll find out tomorrow. I'll do my best," my mom said.

The doorbell rang again. I answered the door. It was Juan.

"Hi Juan. C'mon in," I said.

"And there is my second son," my dad joked. "How goes it today Juan?"

"Stellar as always Mr. Miller," Juan said, shaking my dad's hand.

"Well, we've gotta go right away Dad," I said.

"Alright you guys. Have a good meeting," my mom smiled. "I will let you know in the morning what my company says about investigating."

"Thanks Mrs. M," Veronica said, hugging my mom."

"I won't be late. I should be home by ten or so," I yelled out, while walking down the front sidewalk.

"I just LOVE your parents Marcus!" Veronica said.

"Well, they love you too, you know," I stated.

We raced over to Dezzy's and knocked on the door. Two seconds later, Dezzy answered, out of breath from running up the stairs.

"Hi guys!" Dezzy said. "Let's go down to the family room."

We walked down the stairs and sat at various chairs around the large, sprawling room before us.

"Alright, I have all the equipment. We should check it all out and make sure we have the new batteries installed, if they need to be," Dez said.

"Yeah, and give it a good test to make sure everything's in good working condition," Veronica said.

We passed around all the equipment and found everything in good working order.

"You know, I think that we should bring extra batteries too. Last time we did a big case, at the Rutledge place, when an entity appeared, it drained our batteries for energy," I said. "And it needs energy to manifest itself."

"I have a ton of batteries at home Marcus. I'll bring all of them," Juan said.

"That's great Juan, but what I really want to know is what you two have been experiencing the last two days," Veronica said impatiently. "And what does this have to do with the stadium."

"Yeah, me too!" said Dez.

"Well, remember when we told you about Johnny the bus driver, and what he said to us?" I said.

The girls nodded.

"We went to the bus stop after school that day ready to ask him some questions like we discussed, but when we got there, a different bus driver was driving and she told us that there was no such person driving a bus in our district!" I explained.

"What?" Dez said.

"Yeah. Apparently, we were talking to a ghost named Johnny all along," Juan said.

"And then, later in the day, a Fedex driver dropped off an envelope for me that had this message in it," I said, showing the note to the group.

"Yeah, and the Fedex drivers name was Johnny!" Juan blurted out.

"Geez, bizarre," Veronica said.

"That's not all," Juan nervously laughed. "We went to the library to research the old stadium. When we got there, the librarian at the front desk answered some questions for us. His name was also Johnny! He gave us precise years to research and seemed to know more than he let on."

"Yeah," I agreed. "And then, in a flash, he was gone right before our eyes. It was like he never existed."

"Wow. What the Hell?" Veronica said. "Who is this Johnny?"

"Well, we think it's Johnny 'The Rocket' Espinosa, who was killed in a car crash many years ago.

"The baseball player? Why is he communicating with you?" Dez asked.

"I'm not sure. Maybe it's because he knows that we can communicate with spirits," I responded. "In every message we've received, this Johnny tells us that we need to help them, to do it for them, and do it quickly."

"We did find out that a man killed a woman and her lover in 1932 in the concession stand area," Juan explained. "The killer was her husband."

"Wow, how awful," Dez gasped.

"So we think that the ghosts of the dead are at the stadium, and Johnny is telling us that we need to help them pass on to the afterlife," Juan explained.

"That makes sense. And we need to do this quickly before the stadium is torn down?" Veronica questioned.

"We think so," I responded.

"This totally makes sense," Dez agreed. "I wonder if Johnny 'The Rocket' knew this unfortunate trio?"

"Yeah. Why would Johnny care about these three?" I asked. "And why hasn't Johnny, himself, moved on to the afterlife?"

"Maybe, after Johnny passed, he met them as ghosts and is trying to help them," Juan said. "And Johnny can't move on until they do?"

We continued our discussion for another hour or so until we all had a firm understanding of what our goal was going to be- helping these three people move on, and then helping Johnny. The next night would be the night that we make 'first contact'.

Our meeting broke up around eight-thirty. We all went back home to get ready for school the next day.

Lying in bed that night, I found myself reaching out to Johnny, talking softly into the darkness that surrounded my bed.

"Johnny. If you can hear me. Um...I mean, if you are here with me, can you make a noise so that I know? I want to communicate with you."

Nothing happened. I got up and walked over to my dresser grabbing my audio recording device.

"Johnny. If you are here, speak into the device in my hand. I will be able to hear you if you talk," I said.

I layed there on my bed waiting for something to happen. A very cool, slight breeze gently blew through my room. It gave me 'the chills' up and down my spine and a light-headed feeling. I checked the window in my room. It was closed and locked. My fan was off and the door was shut tight. I stood by my bed and continued to talk out loud.

"Are you here Johnny? Is that you?" I asked. "Speak into this device. I'll be able to hear you."

No response could be heard.

"If you are Johnny, can you tell me if the people you want me to help are the ones that were killed in the stadium back in 1932?"

There was no response, but I still felt as if I was being watched as I sat on the bed. I waited a few minutes asking a few more questions before shutting off the recorder.

I rewound the recorder back to the beginning and played it back so I could hear possible responses to my questions. My questions began...

"Johnny, if you are here, speak into the device in my hand. I will be able to hear you if you talk."

A very inaudible response could be heard through some static white noise. It sounded like a whisper.

"*Help...(static)... stadium...(static)...us,*" the voice responded.

I could barely make it out. The voice sounded almost childlike, and very faint. My next recorded question received a very simple answer.

"Are you here Johnny? Is that you?" I asked. "Speak into this device. I'll be able to hear you."

"*Can't...(static)... Johnny...(static)...,*" *the voice responded.*

"If you are Johnny, can you tell me if the people you want me to help are the ones that were killed in the stadium back in 1932?" I asked on the recording.

"*(static)...Edgar...Joe...(static)...help,*" was the response.

"Holy crap!" I said aloud. "Who is Edgar Joe, or Edgar and Joe, and how does this relate to Johnny? And more importantly, why are they in my bedroom?"

I proceeded to ask many more questions over the next 15 minutes but garnered no response.

Feeling quite shaken by this latest development, I text Juan to get his take on what transpired.

'Juan, ur not going to believe this,' I text. *'I was checking EVP's* (Electronic Voice Phenomenon) *in my room just now and I got a clear response, with static in between. The response had to do with Edgar Joe, or Edgar and Joe, and then it said help.'*

'Edgar Joe?' Juan text. *'How does that relate to Johnny.'*

'No effen clue Juan.' I responded.

'Were either of the men killed in 1932 named Edgar Joe?' Juan asked.

'No' I text. *'Not even close.'*

'Were any of the deaths at the stadium in 1931 named Edgar Joe?' Juan asked.

'Nope' I responded. *'I think we have another case here. Maybe someone died in my house named Edgar Joe? This might not have anything to do with Johnny.'*

'Did you try and keep the conversation going Marcus?' Juan asked.

'I did, for another 20 minutes, but there were no further responses,' I replied.

'Holy crap!' Juan text.

'I think we should concentrate on the stadium for now. Let's put Edgar and Joe on the back burner for a later date,' I text.

'I agree. Let's try to make sense of that later,' Juan agreed. *'It's going to be a late night tomorrow. I need some sleep. Later.'*

'That's easy for you to say Juan, lol,' I responded. *'How many ghosts are in my room now? You think I'm going to be able to sleep. They're probably having a party as we speak'.*

'Lol. See ya tomorrow Marcus', Juan text.

'Later'.

It's no wonder I lacked sleep, I thought. *Between texting about ghosts and other school related things, I was up way too late every night. I was getting only five or six hours of sleep each day. Mr. Johnson, my ninth grade Health teacher, always told us that high schoolers needed at least nine hours of sleep a night. I'm well short of that,* I thought, as I laid my phone on the nightstand and punched my pillow into just the right shape.

I laid my head down, looked around the room and then pulled my covers up to just under my chin.

'*Tomorrow is the day that we get some answers,*' I thought. "Johnny," I said aloud. "We'll see you tomorrow night!"

Chapter 5

AN UNEXPECTED TRAGEDY

When I woke the next morning, I had one thing on my mind, the old Woodticks Stadium. I trotted down the stairs in a rather upbeat mood after getting ready for school. My parents were already at the table eating breakfast, scanning their phones for the latest news and emails of the day.

"Good morning! What's for breakfast today?" I asked.

My mood was obviously very bright and cheery, extremely unusual for me in the morning.

"Good morning to you Marcus. You certainly are happy and cheerful today," my mom said.

"Could this change in attitude be about the Woodticks Stadium, by any chance?" my dad asked.

"Damn right it is Dad!" I boldly answered.

Swearing of any kind was strictly forbidden in our house. I was surprised by my candor.

"Marcus, say that word again and you won't be going anywhere tonight or the next two weeks," my dad shot back quickly.

"Sorry Dad," I said. "We all swear so much at school, I forget when I'm home sometimes."

"That's all well and good Marcus, but not at home, okay?" my mom asked. "By the way, I will text you today on your lunch about getting permission to ghost hunt at the stadium tonight."

"Great Mom. We really appreciate it," I responded.

"If this works out for you Marcus, I want to know what you find during the investigation," my dad said.

"Oh yeah Dad. I will happily share our findings," I responded.

"Great," my dad said. "You know, I'm a huge baseball fan. This peaks my interest."

"Yeah, I know," I agreed. "We are all pretty stoked for this."

The school bus was just a couple of minutes away. I hurried through a bowl of cereal, grabbed my coat and pack, and then took off for school.

The morning bus ride seemed to drag on forever, as did my morning classes. The morning always moved slowly when I was excited for something later in the day. The phone call from my mom is what I was looking forward to today.

As fourth hour ended, my phone buzzed in my front jeans pocket. I took it out and glanced at the screen. It was my mom!

'Hi Honey,' my mom text. 'Believe it or not, I got permission from my boss for you to investigate tonight.'

I just couldn't believe it. This kind of stuff never works out for me. I immediately texted back.

'Wow Mom! Thank you so much,' I replied.

'You're welcome Marcus,' she responded. 'See you at dinner.'

'Bye,' I text, running down the hallway to meet up with the rest of the Para Troupers for lunch.

I ran into the lunch room and saw Juan sitting at the end of a long bench on the first table. I ran over and sat across from him, bursting with excitement at my news.

"Juan!" I said.

"Hey man, what's up?" Juan asked.

"My mom got permission for us to investigate tonight!" I shot back.

"What? Awesomeness!" Juan shouted.

"Oh, here come the girls," I said. "Hey, guess who got permission to investigate tonight at the stadium?"

"What? No way!" Veronica shouted.

"That's awesome!" said Dez, sitting down next to Veronica.

"Wow, I know. I did not expect it would be this easy," I laughed.

Dez, always thinking logically, suggested that we send my mom's boss a thank you message.

"Great idea Dezzy," I said. "I will text my mom for his email address."

I took out my phone and text my mom. She responded back immediately.

'Hi Marcus. I'm happy that this worked out for you. My boss's email address is EdgarJoe1932@gmail.com.'

I looked at my phone, transfixed by what she wrote.

"Marcus, you okay?" Veronica asked while putting her arm around my shoulders.

"Umm, check out her boss's email address you guys," I said, looking as white as a ghost.

"Holy crap!" Dezzy shouted.

Juan jumped to his feet, knocking the table pretty hard. A drink ten feet down, at the end of the table, tipped over spilling its contents all over the table top and onto the floor.

"What the Hell?" Veronica asked.

"Yeah, I know," I said. "What are the odds that Edgar and Joe are part of his email address?"

"Freak city man!" Juan stated in typical Juan fashion.

"Edgar and Joe must be related somehow to this Woodtick Stadium mystery," Veronica surmised.

"I agree, but how?" I said.

"I think we'll get a lot of answers tonight," Dez stated.

The bell rang for us to leave the lunchroom and go to our next class. We stood up from the table.

"Let's meet at my house tonight at seven," I said. "Can everyone make it?"

Everyone was onboard, so we hurried off to class.

My mind wandered all afternoon. I couldn't concentrate on anything in all of my classes. The Woodticks Stadium took up all the space between my ears. I got an F on my Science quiz in sixth hour and I failed to turn in my English homework in seventh hour.

My performance in school today was very atypical for me, so when the bell rang at the end of the day, I was happy to leave the school and meet up with Juan for the ride home on the bus.

"Hey Marcus, how was your day, man?"

"Oh, you know," I said sarcastically. "Failed a quiz, forgot to turn in homework due today. So kind of a crappy day."

"I hear ya Marcus." Juan said, shaking his head. "I had a poor day myself. The good thing about school today, is that it's in the past. Let's talk about something really important. What do you make of that email address your mom sent us today?" Juan asked.

"I don't know man," I responded. "But I think tonight will bring some much needed answers at the stadium."

Just then, Timmy, a boy with a reputation as the ninth grade bully, poked his head between ours and interrupted our conversation.

""Hey you guys, are you talking about the Woodticks Stadium?" he asked.

"Hey Timmy," I said. "Yeah, we're just mad that it's going to be torn down next week."

"What's going on tonight?" Timmy asked. "Are you guys investigating the place?"

"Well, we want to," I responded, not wanting to give him any information.

"Cool man," he said. "You may run into something very bad there, like the devil or something."

Timmy laughed, swatted my head pretty hard with his hand and then sat back down into his seat, immediately irritating the boy next to him.

Juan leaned over to me and whispered.

"Oh great. Now Timmy knows about this?"

"Yeah, that's all we need," I said. "A bully with a penchant for trouble."

The bus dropped us off at our stop, and we continued home by foot.

"What kind of trouble do you think Timmy is going to give us?" I asked.

"I don't know," said Juan. "He's a big bully, but he's younger than us. We can handle anything he dishes out."

"He may be younger, but he's a good 6 inches taller and 50 pounds heavier than us Juan," I responded.

"He's no match for our toned torsos Marcus," Juan laughed.

"Yeah right," I smiled.

We reached Juan's house.

"See you tonight Marcus," Juan said. "Seven o'clock sharp!"

I walked the rest of the way home, turning in to my backyard through our old wooden gate.

"Hey Miller!" came a voice from the alley.

It was Timmy.

"Hey Timmy," I said. "What's up?"

"I want to go to the stadium with you guys tonight," he said.

"Geez Timmy, our group got special permission to go from the demolition contractor," I explained. "Only our group was approved."

"That's alright I guess," Timmy said. "Maybe I can go with you guys on another investigation."

"Yeah, sure Timmy," I said. "We'll let you know."

"Great. See you in school Monday Marcus."

"See ya," I responded.

For just a second, I saw beyond his large, bullying exterior. He seemed very interested in the paranormal and very interested in going with our group on an investigation.

'Maybe, I thought, *there was something decent, buried deeply in this kid after all.*'

I went in the house, ate supper, gathered my audio recording device and EMF (Electro Magnetic Frequency) meter and went to the family room to watch some television before the group arrived. An electromagnetic frequency meter measures the amount of magnetic energy in the air. Ghostly entities use this energy to manifest themselves. So the larger the amount of magnetic energy around, the greater the chances of ghosts appearing.

The front doorbell rang. I ran up the stairs and answered the door. Veronica, Juan and Dez were all standing on the top step, waiting impatiently for the investigation to begin.

"Hi guys!" I said. "Let me grab my stuff and I will be ready in just a second. C'mon in."

They all stood by the door waiting as my mom approached to say hi.

"Greetings ghost hunters," she said to the group. "Are you guys ready for this?"

I ran back to join the group at the door.

"We are so ready for this!" Veronica answered.

"I just want you to be very careful, and safe, as you investigate," my mom said. "No one gets hurt! Okay?"

"You got it Mrs. M!" Juan said.

We left the house and piled into Juans car for the short ride to the ballpark.

"My mom is such a worry wart," I said.

"I think its cute Marcus. There are many parents that I know that don't care so much about their kids and what they do," Veronica said.

"True that Veronica," Juan chimed in.

"You've got some pretty cool parents Marcus," Dez agreed.

We pulled up to the old parking lot that ran adjacent to the old Woodticks Stadium. Juan parked his car next to the gate. We grabbed all of the equipment and made our way into the ballpark grounds area.

"It sure was nice of the demolition company to leave this gate unlocked for us Marcus," Veronica said.

"Yeah it was," I agreed.

"We're so used to sneaking in to the stadium, it seems weird to enter the normal way," Juan said.

"It sure was nice of the demolition company to leave this gate unlocked for us Marcus," Veronica said.

"Yeah it was," I agreed.

"We're so used to sneaking in to the stadium, it seems weird to enter the normal way," Juan said.

We all laughed.

"Okay. These grounds are quite large. We don't ever want to be in a position where we are alone investigating, so why don't we pair up," I directed. "Veronica and I can take the grandstand area and Juan and Dez take the outfield and locker room areas."

"Dezzy and I can start with the camera, the video camera and the temperature gauge," Juan said.

"Marcus and I can use the EMF gauge and the audio recorder," Veronica said.

"Maybe half way through our investigation we can switch off and use the other equipment?" Dez suggested.

"Great idea Dezzy," agreed Veronica.

"Okay then, you guys go that way (pointing to the outfield), and we'll go that way (pointing to the grandstand)," I explained. "Keep your cell phones on and communicate as needed. Let's meet back here in two hours sharp."

"Alright, here we go," Veronica said. "See ya later guys."

"See ya. Good luck," Juan said.

Veronica and I started toward the grandstand. The weather was warm, and there was a slight breeze swirling gently in the grandstand area, just behind home plate. Not a sound could be heard throughout the stadium.

"What a perfect night to do this, huh Marcus?" Veronica whispered, gently slipping her arm through mine and holding my hand as we walked.

"Yeah. It's a perfect night isn't it?" I asked.

"Do you smell popcorn Marcus?" Veronica asked.

"Yeah, I do," I answered. "Weird. The smell may be in the wooden seats from all those years of popcorn being consumed during games."

As we very slowly walked up the aisle way right behind home plate, we heard very faint footsteps above us on the rooftop. The old, rotting boards that the magnificent structure was made up of seemed to move and sway in the gentle breeze that surrounded us.

"Those footsteps seem to be following us as we move, getting louder as we go," I said. "Maybe the wind is making the boards sound like footsteps."

As we stood there, listening to the footsteps about 75 feet above us, a small cup of popcorn fell from the roof and landed on Veronica's shoulder.

"What the Hell was that?" Veronica asked.

"I have no idea," I answered.

There was a loud laugh echoing through the grandstand area. It seemed to be emanating from the rooftop. We looked up.

"Hey, who's up there?" Veronica shouted. "Are you nuts?"

A head poked through a hole in the roof and whoever it was was laughing hard at us.

"Ha! I sure made you scared, didn't I?" the voice asked.

"Timmy? Is that you?" I yelled.

"It sure is!" he yelled back.

"Get down from there!" Veronica yelled. "There's rotting boards up there. Are you crazy?"

Before Timmy could answer, his left foot broke through the rooftop and he began to slip through the hole. He screamed.

"HELP!" he yelled. "I can't hang on!"

I looked around the grandstand and saw a stairway in the back that looked like it went to the roof. I ran up the grandstand stairs as fast as I could to get to the back staircase.

"I'll call 911!" shouted Veronica.

I began to run up the back staircase when I heard a sickening scream. It was Veronica. I glanced back just in time to see Timmy falling from the hole in the roof. His body came crashing into the first level seats. I ran down the stairs as fast as I could. We ran up to where he landed. His head was over the back of a seat and his body was twisted over the front of another. There was blood pouring from an unseen part of his body.

"Oh my God Timmy," Veronica cried.

I took off my coat and applied pressure to where I thought the bleeding was coming from. I was crying as well. I had never seen anything like this in my life. Sirens were blaring in the distance as we felt helpless in the face of tragedy.

Timmy slightly moved his head toward us and spoke his last words.

"Marcus, I think we could have been friends," he gasped.

His head turned to the side, his body trembled and jerked slightly and then his eyes closed. I frantically talked to him, pleading that he stay awake. I felt so powerless. We cried and held his hands until the emergency crew came, but he was gone. This bully of a kid had made a connection with us, maybe the only connection he ever had, and now his life was tragically taken.

By the time Juan and Dezzy had arrived at the scene after hearing Veronica scream, Timmy's body was being removed by the EMT's. We explained what had happened to them. This was devastating for our group.

We sat down in the grandstand, just a few seats down from where Timmy fell. We were approached by a couple of Spider Lake cops. Our hearts were heavy.

"Hey kids, what exactly happened here?" one of the policemen asked. "You were all here when he fell, right?"

We tried to compose ourselves.

"Veronica and I saw it happen," I said. "Juan and Dezzy were in the outfield area and saw nothing but the aftermath."

"Yeah, we got permission from the demolition company to do some exploring tonight," Veronica explained. "Timmy was not approved to be here. He's not part of our group."

"How were you approved to be here?" the policeman asked.

I pulled out our written permission and showed it to the officer.

"Okay, very good," he said. "I would like your phone numbers and addresses in case we need to contact you for anything."

We supplied our information, still in shock from the incident.

"Okay, thanks kids," the other cop said. "Why don't you guys take off and get home. We'll be contacting your parents informing them of what happened."

"Thank you sir," Dezzy said.

"Yeah thanks," Juan said.

We stood up and slowly walked toward the exit, deciding to tell our parents right away about Timmy's tragedy when we got home. We were more silent than we have ever been, not saying one word as we entered the parking lot.

Before we reached Juan's car, Dez turned and looked at the creepy, dark stadium with a puzzled look on her face.

"Whats up Dezzy?" Veronica asked. "Did you leave something there?"

"No," she responded. "Besides the two cops, we were the last to leave the stadium right?" Dez sniffled.

"Yeah, we were!" I answered.

"Don't you hear that guys?" Dez asked.

"I do," shouted Juan, twirling around looking at the grandstand. "It sounds like someone crying, a kid, like they're hurt or something."

"There was no other kids in there though," I said. "Oh wait, I hear it too!", turning my ear in the stadium's direction.

We stood in the parking lot, motionless and silent.

"Hey, what's that?" Veronica asked pointing at a shimmering, faint light that seemed to be falling from the sky into the stadium.

No one could respond. We stood there, mouths wide open, eyes locked on the light.

"Hey, look at that!" Juan shouted.

There was a very small orb rising up from the bleachers. It seemed to meet the light falling from the black night sky.

In a quick flash of brilliant light, the two lights burst into the heavens at an incredible speed.

I looked at Veronica.

"Timmy?" I asked.

Veronica looked at me with tears in her eyes and simply nodded yes.

This was the second time that we had witnessed an event like this. Old Man Rutledge, in the previous summer, had passed the same way.

"Wow!" said Juan. "I never get tired of seeing that."

"He's in a much better place, that's for sure," said Dez, as we stood arm in arm.

"He was not a very happy person here on Earth," I said. "Maybe he'll find happiness wherever he is headed."

Everyone nodded in agreement as the lights disappeared high in the heavens.

We left in Juan's car and went home. It had been a quick, but tragic night.

Because of Timmy's accidental death at the stadium, the demolition of the sight was delayed 30 days while police investigated the death.

Our parents new that we had nothing to do with Timmy's actions so they had no reason to punish us. They did, however, forbid us from going to the sight again, deeming that it was an unsafe structure.

But our work was not complete. There were still souls to save at the stadium and an unfinished investigation. We had decisions to make.

Chapter 6

OPPORTUNITY KNOCKS

Residents in the town of Spider Lake were shocked by Timmy's death, spawning more calls for the old stadium's destruction as soon as possible.

For several days, schools provided counseling services to students and families having a hard time coping with the tragedy of a fellow classmate.

It took about a week after Timmy's death before I had the nerve to approach my parents for another shot at investigating the crumbling structure. My dad seemed more open to allowing it, but my mom was adamant against our exploring any further, citing the obvious safety concerns.

Following the discussion with my parents, I went to bed, saddened and dejected. I slept hard that night, but still awoke the next day, with a clogged head, feeling tired and looking unkempt. I plopped down on the couch in the living room and turned on some cartoons, with Timmy's fate still fresh on my mind.

"Good morning Marcus," my dad said as he came down the stairs, finding a seat on the recliner next to me.

"Morning Dad," I responded.

"Marcus, I know that you're probably not in a mood to talk this morning, but I have something that I want to say to you," my dad blurted out.

I could feel a deep tongue lashing coming from my dad. He was good at providing teachable moments for Courtney and I. My eyes couldn't help but roll up into my head as I waited for his lecture.

"This may surprise you," he continued, "But your mother and I talked for a long time last night and have decided to allow you to investigate the stadium again."

My eyes widened. My head turned quickly toward my dad. My mouth was open wide.

"What did you say?" I stammered.

"We have decided to let you investigate the stadium again," he repeated.

"Really?" I asked again, looking for more confirmation.

"Well, we know that Timmy came on his own volition," my dad explained. "We know that you told him that the Para Troupers were the only group allowed to investigate, and he came anyway. You had no control over that. You also knew what to do in the face of an emergency. We are actually quite proud of the way that you reacted throughout the whole ordeal. Therefore, we have decided that you have done nothing wrong and deserve another chance."

I hurried over to my dad and gave him a big hug.

"Thanks Dad," I said. "We will not disappoint you or anyone else. We are very careful. Safety is always our first concern."

"I realize, and appreciate, that. Furthermore Marcus, we are going to call the parents of the other Para Troupers and let them know of our decision," he said.

"Wow, thanks Dad!" I said.

"Your mother and I have complete confidence in you," he continued.

I thanked him again and ran upstairs to let my friends know.

It's funny how things have a way of turning out when you do the right thing most of the time, I thought.

My dad called the other parents that morning. Veronica's and Dezzy's parents were onboard too. Juan's parents saw it much differently and continued to ban Juan from the ballpark. I understood their concerns, but a frustrated Juan did not.

'*Well, what my parents don't know won't kill them*,' Juan texted to me later that morning.

'*Well, I can't tell you what to do Juan. That's up to you*,' I replied. '*Either way, we are fine with your decision. I hoped your parents would understand.*'

'*When are we going again Marcus?*' Juan texted.

'*We are doing it again tonight*,' I replied.

'*Sweet. I'll be there Marcus.*'

'*Okay. Why don't we meet in the same parking lot as last time Juan, at say, eight o'clock?*'

'*Sounds like a plan. See you then*," replied Juan.

I can't say that I agreed with Juan's decision, but we always did everything together. It would've felt strange not having him around for the investigation. I called the girls and informed them of the meeting time and location. We were set for the investigation of the old Woodticks Stadium- Part Two.

After completing chores and homework all afternoon, I showered and met my family at the dinner table at exactly six o'clock.

"So tonight's the big night Marcus?" my mom asked.

"Yup. I feel good about this one," I responded.

"Well, good luck and be safe," my dad sternly said. "I don't want to hear of any more injuries, or God forbid, worse happening."

"You have my word Dad," I promised.

"I want to go with Marcus," my sister Courtney spouted off.

"ABSOLUTELY NOT!" my mom responded loudly.

"It's stupid anyway," Courtney said, turning her head and folding her arms.

"Yeah right!" I yelled back at her.

"Okay kids. That's enough," my mom said with a raised voice.

My sister drove me crazy. I could barely handle being around her sometimes. I cleaned up my dishes, grabbed my equipment and headed out the door for the ballpark.

It was a ten block walk from my house, so I was happy when Veronica met me part way. She had a way of calming me in the face of stressful situations.

"Hi Marcus," Veronica said smiling.

She leaned over and gave me a kiss on the cheek and held onto my arm as we walked. I instantly relaxed and held onto her hand firmly.

"Hi Veronica," I said. "I am so looking forward to doing this tonight."

"Me too Marcus," Veronica responded. "That's too bad that Juan can't come too."

"Oh no, he'll be there," I explained.

"Really?" Veronica questioned.

"Yeah. He's going despite his parents' wishes," I said.

"Oh boy. It'll be nice having him there of course, but if anything goes wrong for us, he'll be in big trouble," Veronica said.

"Tell me about it," I agreed. "Juan's parents have been known to be the strictest parents around, especially if their children misbehave."

We continued walking and arrived at the stadium in just a few short minutes. Juan was already there. Dez arrived a few minutes later.

"Are you sure you want to do this Juan?" I asked.

"Hell's yeah," he responded. "I would never let what my parents say dictate what I do, at least most of the time."

"All right then. Here's the plan," I said. "I think it should be the same as last week."

"Ha," Juan laughed. "It took you a long time to come up with that I bet."

We all laughed and entered the stadium. It felt as if we were starting out with a fresh set of eyes, looking for anything that we could find that may help us solve the mystery. They included sounds, voices, smells, temperature changes, breezes, mists forming, audio recordings, EMF meter changes and picture evidence. We needed to stay alert at all times. What might be thought of as a very minor observation may be the clue that we need. We couldn't ignore anything.

"I have to admit Marcus, it's pretty creepy being here today," Veronica said. "I mean, they just cleaned off Timmy's blood yesterday from the seats."

"Yeah, I know," I responded. "He just died right there," I said, pointing at the section where he had passed.

"Do you think that his spirit might be here as well Marcus?" Veronica asked.

"No." I answered. "I think it's pretty clear that we saw his spirit leave the ballpark last week."

"Why don't we do an EVP session right here?" Veronica suggested.

"It's as good a place as any," I agreed.

We sat in the fifth row, in the section just up from the first base dugout. I pulled out the audio recording device that we had and Veronica turned on the EMF device that measures magnetic electrical energy. We began to ask questions.

"Hi. My name is Marcus and this is Veronica," I said.

"Hi," Veronica said with a slight wave into the air.

"We are trying to communicate with Johnny 'The Rocket' Espinosa and anyone that may have died here over the years," I said aloud. "Is anyone here with us tonight?"

We waited a few seconds to give the entities a chance to respond, before Veronica asked the next question.

"If Johnny is here, could you please respond by knocking on this pillar on the count of three like I am doing?" Veronica asked.

She leaned over to one of the pillars next to us and knocked three times very loudly, hoping to garner a response. No response could be heard.

"Let's go back to the beginning of our questions and see if there's been any responses so far," I suggested.

I turned on the audio recorder and replayed our first two questions. There was no answer at all.

"Let's try over there by the third base dugout Veronica," I directed.

We slowly walked to the other side of the grandstand and sat down just a few rows up from the dugout where Jennifer Stone was killed by the line drive from Cody 'The Hammer' Johnson and that double murder/suicide took place over eighty-five years ago. It was still obvious where the city removed the blood splattered cement from the area and replaced it with new concrete. The area covered a good 75 square feet.

I took out my audio recorder and asked more questions.

"I would like to speak to Johnny 'The Rocket' Espinosa," I said. "Johnny, are you here?"

We waited a few seconds before I asked another question.

"Johnny, we have been seeing signs of your presence all over the town lately. We've heard you talk to us while we're in bed at night. What can we do to help? What do you need from us?" I asked.

"Marcus! Oh My God! Look!" Veronica shouted.

The EMF gauge was going crazy. Normally, the light is green, meaning that energy levels are normal or non-existent. The lights on the gauge had passed through green, yellow and orange and were even into the red-zone, the highest level possible.

"We are sensing that you are here Johnny," I said.

The lights on the EMF gauge went down to green.

"If you stand next to this meter we've got, you can verify to us that you are here and that you're Johnny," I explained.

"If you are Johnny, can you make the lights go up to red again?" I asked.

The lights immediately went up to red.

"Marcus, we are communicating with 'The Rocket'!" Veronica said. "Unbelievable!"

I looked at Veronica and smiled.

"Johnny, please tell us what you need us for," I directed. "If you speak into the recorder device, I will be able to hear you."

The EMF gauge was maintaining it's red level. I rewound the recording device to see if we got answers. I hit play.

'(large amounts of strange static noises)...*wait*...(static continues)...'

"Did you hear that Veronica?" I asked.

"Yeah! Did it say '*wait*'?"

"Yeah! We got a one word response," I said.

"Hmmm...wait for what, and how long?" Veronica questioned.

We sat there for a few minutes waiting for something to happen. I called Juan and told him to come to where we were right away. Juan and Dezzy arrived just a few minutes later.

"What's up guys?" Dez asked us.

We reviewed what happened so far, with them.

"Sweet!" hollered Juan.

"Juan, keep it down man," I said. "We don't want to miss anything."

"Wow! Marcus! Look!" Veronica yelled.

The EMF gauge was going crazy.

Dezzy looked down at the temperature gauge. It read forty-eight degrees.

"The temperature is dropping," said Dez. "It's sixty-five outside, yet the temperature around us dropped to forty-eight!"

"Something's going down!" Juan loudly said.

"Remember, entities need an enormous amount of energy to materialize into full-bodied ghosts, or appear to the naked eye," I explained.

We held onto our equipment, huddling together for warmth. The wind in the stadium was increasing. Something was about to happen. It was obvious.

"The EMF gauge is dead," said Veronica. "Batteries are drained of energy."

"Yup, the temperature gauge is out too!" yelled out Dezzy.

The wind began to blow the infield dirt, on the field, into mini dust tornados.

"Look! In front of the third base dugout!" I screamed, pointing in the direction of a swirling mist out on the field. "It's an entity forming!"

"I can't make it out," Veronica yelled out. "What is it?"

The noise from the strong winds was deafening.

Dezzy was holding her hair off her face when she screamed out.

"It looks like a ballplayer! Number one on the jersey! I can't make out the name on the back!"

"MY GOD!" I yelled out.

"What's wrong?!" Veronica screamed.

I looked at Juan. He reciprocated.

"It's 'The Rocket!' I screamed out. "He had the number one jersey number!"

We stood there, hanging on to each other. All of our equipment, and phones, were dead.

"One entity shouldn't be able to knock off all of our equipment!" I yelled. "Unless there are multiple entities trying to materialize!"

A thunderous, low pitched, but very loud, noise shook our feet. It felt like an earthquake. We covered our ears. There was nothing we could do except stand there. The wind and the noise was so deafening, we couldn't hear each other anymore.

And then, in a split second, everything stopped. The wind was non-existent. The noises that we heard were gone. The 'Rockets' entity had disappeared. It was a stunning reversal of conditions. So disturbing, that we just sat down where we were to recover.

"Holy crap!" Juan said, breaking the quiet. "We saw Espinosa's ghost, but just before he finished materializing, something exploded over the stadium, suppressing him and everything else. Wow!"

"Yeah, what the Hell was that?" I added. "It shook my body to its core. I thought the stadium might collapse!"

"Hey, check all the equipment," Veronica added. "Is there anything working, or is it all dead?"

"All is dead," Dez said.

"Juan, how about all your backup batteries?" I asked.

After pulling dead ones out of the equipment and replacing them with new ones Juan had bad news.

"All dead, every last one of them!" he responded.

"Wow, whatever that was, is so large, and powerful, it literally destroyed every battery that we had," I explained. "Amazing."

"We are left without any equipment now," said Dez.

"Yeah. We're going to have to return tomorrow and try again," I said. "I just have no idea what we're dealing with now."

"It seems, however, that all the action is on the third base side of the grandstand," said Juan.

"Excellent observation Juan," I said. "We saw Johnny so we know that he's here. Being it's the third base side of the grandstand, it could be that we're dealing with Jennifer Stone who got hit with the baseball, or we're dealing with the murder-suicide tragedy."

"Neither one seems like it would be able to produce that amount of energy though," Veronica noticed.

"You're right Veronica," I agreed. "Maybe what produced that amount of energy was all of them combined."

"Or, maybe it was truly an entity so evil, so bad, that it has amassed an enormous amount of negative energy for all the bad things they have done," said Dezzy.

"Wow, I never thought of that Dezzy," said Veronica. "Good call."

"I'm not sure about you guys, but I'm ready to do this again. Can everyone do tomorrow night, same time?" I asked.

We all could.

"Excellent!" I said.

We had no choice but to leave the stadium and go home for some well-deserved rest. We weren't sure what we were in for, but we had an investigation to do. We had many entities to help and a very large evil entity to deal with. Onward!

Chapter 7

REGROUPING FOR THE HUNT

We were exhausted. Not only did something drain all the batteries that we had, but it left all of us zapped of energy. When I got home, I went right up to bed and fell asleep in my clothes, shoes and all.

I awoke with the sound of Courtney talking on the phone to Veronica's sister, Rachel. I glanced over at my clock. It was eleven o'clock.

Wow, my parents let me sleep in on a Saturday morning? I thought to myself.

I threw my covers aside and sat up in bed, checking my phone for messages. There were none.

Wow, strange, I thought. *I always had friends texting at all hours.*

I walked over to my dresser and put on some clothes before heading to the bathroom. I always brushed my teeth before I did anything else in the morning. I could overhear Courtney's conversation with Rachel from her bedroom down the hallway.

"Yeah, I know," Courtney said into the phone. "I can't wait Rachel. This is going to be so cool!"

She sat on her bed smiling into the phone as she listened.

"Yeah, okay. Six o'clock then. See ya," she said.

She came bursting through her door into the hallway, blowing past the bathroom.

"Hey Courtney!" I yelled down the hallway. "What do you guys have going on tonight?" I asked.

"None of your business," she replied.

"Yeah, well so much for caring, I guess," I yelled back.

I worried that Rachel and Courtney were going to do their own special investigation at the ballpark and get into trouble.

I finished brushing my teeth and headed downstairs, texting as I went.

"Good morning Marcus," my mom smiled.

"Morning Mom," I answered.

"Geez, they still haven't answered my texts," I complained.

"They're probably quite tired like you were last night," my mom said. "I asked how it went last night when you got home, and you just walked right past me and fell asleep in your bed."

"Yeah, sorry about that," I apologized. "We were beat. All went well, but we were just zapped of energy."

"That's okay," she answered. "Did you finish your investigation?"

"Unfortunately no. All of our batteries went dead. Luckily, most of them are rechargeable batteries, or this could get quite expensive," I admitted.

"We are going to go again tonight, if that's okay?" I asked.

"It is. Just be careful," she said.

My phone began to 'ding', meaning I had a couple of text messages. I grabbed it and walked into the living room to respond.

'Marcus, I think that we should talk with Mrs. Miller this afternoon and get her take on what happened last night,' Veronica text.

'Fine with me Veronica,' I replied. *'I also want to find out why my mom's boss has Edgar and Joe in his email address.'*

'Yes, that would be interesting to find out,' she text.

'I'll pick you up about one o'clock. Is that good for you?' I asked.

'Yeah. Great. See ya then,' she replied.

"Hey Mom?" I yelled into the kitchen.

"Yah Marcus," she responded.

"Do you know why your boss, Mr. Donskey, has EdgarJoe in his email address?" I asked.

"Well, that's his first and middle name," she replied. "Edgar Joe Donskey."

"Really," I said, rubbing my chin like a good detective should do when trying to solve a case. "Interesting."

My mom chuckled seeing my response.

"Is there something else on your mind about his name Marcus?" she questioned.

"Well, Edgar and Joe were names that I heard recently when I was trying to get to sleep at night," I said. "The words were verbally told to me, but no one was there in the room."

"Wow. What a weird coincidence," my mom said.

"Yeah, tell me about it," I agreed.

I sat at the table and enjoyed a good breakfast before setting out with Veronica to speak with Mrs. Ardene Miller.

Mrs. Miller was the longtime Spider Lake expert on ghostly entities, and a friend of ours. She was enormously helpful in solving the Rutledge case from last summer. Even though she was officially retired, she found herself smack dab in the middle of that case, getting stabbed by an evil entity when it sought her out for helping us. Her recovery was slow, over six months long, because of her advancing age and unwillingness to remain inactive to help heal. She was a very feisty woman indeed.

I got to Veronica's and approached the front door. She was waiting for me and came out right away.

"Hey Marcus," she said, giving me a hug and a gentle pat on my lower back. "This case is really getting intense. I can't wait to see what we can learn from Mrs. Miller."

"Yeah, I know," I said. "Why the huge power loss, and what was that booming noise that shook our feet?"

"That was so cool," Veronica said.

"It may be cool, but it stopped our investigation in its tracks when all the batteries went dead," I responded.

"Hey, did your mom know anything about Edgar Joe and her bosses email address?" Veronica asked.

"Yeah, Edgar is his first name and Joe is his middle name," I answered.

"Hmmm, that's still a weird coincidence, don't ya think Marcus?" she asked.

"Yeah, for sure," I said. "I just can't see any connection yet though, at all."

"Me either," Veronica said. "Oh look, there's Mrs. Miller's house. Let's go."

We approached her front door and rang her very loud doorbell. "DING-DONG!!!"

"Yikes, I forgot how loud that thing is," Veronica said, covering her ears with her hands.

The door slowly opened. We walked over the threshold and into the entryway.

"Hey, good morning children," Mrs. Miller said as she slowly walked in our direction across her expansive living room. "What brings my two favorite young people over to see me today?"

We hugged her as she invited us to sit down and talk.

"I made cookies today. Would you like several?" she asked.

"Sure." I said.

"Thanks Mrs. Miller. You are too kind," Veronica said.

Veronica was very good at the social graces with people older than herself.

"Mmm, oatmeal raisin," I said. "These are delicious."

"Thank you dear," she said. "What can I help you with?"

"Well," said Veronica, "We have a case at the old Woodticks Stadium, and we believe that Johnny 'The Rocket' Espinosa is communicating with us to help some people that were killed at the stadium many years ago."

"I loved watching 'The Rocket' play. He was such a good boy too. What a tragic end. Are you sure it's him?" she asked.

"Yeah. Positive," I said. "We were at the ballpark last night when 'The Rocket' was materializing before us."

"Wow. Fantastic," Mrs. Miller said.

"But then, a very large booming noise happened, shaking our feet as we stood," Veronica explained.

"Yeah, and then every last battery we had went dead at the same time," I said.

"Were all four of you near each other?" she asked us.

"Well, yeah. We were right next to each other," I further explained.

"There's the problem, right there," she continued. If an evil entity is near you, it will suck all the power from anything near it, creating a super-charged entity. Next time you go out, spread yourself around. It can only take the energy near it."

"So it will be weaker because of the lack of energy available?" I asked.

"Exactly," she said.

"I knew that we'd learn something new coming to see you Mrs. Miller," Veronica said. "Thanks for your help."

"You're welcome Dear," Mrs. Miller responded. "Who do you think Johnny wants you to help save?"

"Well, we are concentrating on a double murder and suicide in 1932 and a woman that was killed by a line drive off the bat of Cody 'The Hammer' Johnson, in 1931," I explained.

"You know, not all entities, or spirits, are the result of a killing or a suicide," she explained. "Sometimes a person is attached to something at the stadium, maybe a person or an object, and is transported to the site. Keep your options open and think outside of the box."

"I never thought of that," I admitted.

"Me neither. Thanks for the tip Mrs Miller," Veronica said.

"No problem children. If you need more help, you know where to find me," she said. "I don't get out much anymore."

"Well, we better get back home and get ready for tonight's investigation," Veronica said. "Thanks again for your invaluable help."

"Yes. Thank you so much, and thanks for the cookies," I said, grabbing a couple more for the road.

We hugged our favorite ghost hunter and went back home to prepare for the night ahead, armed with new, and crucial, knowledge to combat evil entities.

Juan and I had all the batteries on chargers today in preparation for this evenings investigation, so when I got home, I made sure that they were ready.

"Yup, all charged and ready," I said to myself.

My phone started to send me notifications again, a whole bunch of them. I grabbed my phone. Veronica had sent seven new messages in the last few minutes.

'Marcus, call me,' said the first text. 'I just talked to Rachel.'

I knew it, I thought. *They were planning on going to the stadium tonight I bet.*

I dialed Veronica and she picked up immediately.

"Hi Marcus," she said.

"Hi V..," I couldn't even finish saying hi when she started to tell me what happened.

"Those little turds," she went on to say. "They were planning on following us tonight and doing their own investigation. Can you believe that? Especially after what happened last year."

"I knew it!" I said. "That's all we would need, a couple of nosy rookies playing with fire. This could be life or death!"

"Exactly," agreed Veronica.

Last year, our little sisters pulled the same thing in the Rutledge Case and it almost cost them, and us, our lives.

"I will talk to my parents about this," I said. "Maybe they can make sure she stays home tonight."

"I'll do the same Marcus," she said. "Hey, I'll see ya tonight at eight o'clock, right?"

"Yup," I answered. "Bye Veronica."

I went downstairs immediately and informed my dad about Courtney's plan. He was not too happy with her idea. I knew that she just wanted to be a part of the excitement, but she was untrained, and a liability for us.

I went to my room and spent the next couple of hours doing homework for Monday. It was going to be a big night tonight. I wanted to lay low for a while.

A text message came through from Dezzy.

'Hey Marcus. Just thinking. All bad things that happened at the stadium happened by the third base dugout, including Timmy. Maybe something is buried under the stadium in that spot?' she text.

'Hmmm. Not a bad idea,' I replied. 'Maybe they built the stadium on some old burial grounds or something?'

'Maybe,' she text. 'There is something about that spot that's bad, that's evil.'

'I agree Dez,' I replied. 'Can't wait for tonight.'

'Me either,' she text. 'See ya tonight Marcus.'

'Later,' I said.

Our minds were working overtime trying to solve this case. No ideas were off the table.

Our house phone began to ring. We were one of the few houses, that I knew of, that still had a house phone.

"I'll get it!" I yelled into the hallway by my bedroom.

"Um, hello?" I said into the phone.

"This must be Marcus," the voice said. "This is Mr. Donskey. Is your mom home?"

"Oh hi Mr. Donskey," I said.

Mr. Donskey was calling to speak to my mom about work matters.

"Sure, I'll get her right away," I said, as I laid the phone down on the hallway table.

I was just about to yell out to her when I had an idea.

"Um, Mr. Donskey?" I asked.

"Yes Marcus?" he said.

"I noticed that your first and middle names are Edgar Joe," I said. "I hope you don't mind me asking, but how did you get your name? Are you named after anybody?"

Mr. Donskey laughed on the other end of the line.

"No, I don't mind at all Marcus," he answered. "I was named after my two uncles Edgar and Joe."

"Are they still living? Are they still around?" I shot back.

"Well, I'm not sure what your interest would be with my uncles, but they died many, many years ago," he said.

"Hmmm," I mumbled.

"Marcus! Was someone on the phone?" my mom yelled up the stairs.

"Yeah Mom," I yelled back. "It's Mr. Donskey for you."

"Okay Marcus, you can hang up now," she said, after picking up the phone in the living room.

I hung up the phone.

That just didn't make any sense, I thought. *His uncles don't have anything to do with the stadium. They probably lived a full life. Why would they want to see me in the middle of the night?*

I finished up my homework, ate dinner, and was soon off to meet the other Para Troupers at the stadium. My conversation with Mr. Donskey was still fresh on my mind as I met up with Juan part way down the block.

"Hey man," Juan said.

"Hey, you remember that Edgar Joe email address that my mom's boss has?" I asked.

"Yeah, what about it?" Juan said.

"Well, I had been trying to figure out if there was a connection with the Edgar Joe in my dream," I explained.

"Yeah?" Juan asked.

"Well, Edgar and Joe were my Mom's bosses uncles. They died years ago," I said. "I think that's a dead end. No connection there."

"Bummer," Juan said. "I thought that was a promising lead."

"Me too," I said. "Oh well, have you got all the charged batteries Juan?"

"Yup, I do," he said.

"Did your parents suspect anything?" I asked.

"Nothing at all," Juan said proudly.

"Alright. Let's meet up with the girls and do this!" I yelled out with my fist in the air.

"Whoo hoo!" Juan yelled. "Watch out evil entities! The Para Troupers are on the job!"

A NEAR DEATH EXPERIENCE

The night was still and eerily quiet. There was no wind. Even the constant hum of cars traveling up and down Arachna Parkway, several blocks away, was non-existent.

"Geez, where is everybody?" Juan asked, breaking the silence of the moment.

"I was just thinking the same thing," I said. "The moon's not even out. It's pitch black out here tonight."

"Yeah, weird," Juan agreed.

We were just a couple of blocks away from the old beautiful stadium and still unable to see its majestic grandstand because of the unexpected darkness.

"I know it's here somewhere Marcus," Juan laughed.

"There it is!" I yelled out, pointing ahead to the grandstand rising into the night sky. "It's a spooky looking piece of history, huh Juan?"

"It sure is Marcus," he answered. "I still can't believe that this beautiful sight will be gone when those apartments are built. Tragic."

"You got that right Juan, my man," I said, slapping Juan square in the middle of his back. "C'mon, let's meet up with the girls."

We jogged the last block and found the girls sitting on a rusty bike stand that was just in front of the old players entrance to the ballpark.

"Hey guys," Veronica blurted out. "You ready?"

"Oh yeah," I said. "I have a feeling that this will be a big night."

"Let's hope we get some answers and help those that need it," Dez said.

We all agreed.

"You know, Dezzy and I were sitting here waiting and thinking," Veronica said.

"Yeah?" I asked.

"We girls want to explore together tonight," she said. "Then you two guys can work together too."

"I'm fine with that," I said. "We all need to keep our cell phones on and communicate often."

"Great," agreed Dez.

"We must stay apart as much as possible," Veronica said. "Remember what Mrs. Miller told us. If we all get too close to each other, an evil entity can use all of the power that we have and create a monstrous entity too hard to handle. By separating, its power is weakened and more manageable."

"Those are words we need to live by," I said.

"Alright, we all ready?" Dez asked.

"Let's go!" Juan yelled.

Juan and I walked through the bleacher entrance where old wooden benches once stood near the first base line. Veronica and Dezzy went through the players entrance with the intention of exploring under the grandstand, looking for possible reasons why so many deaths occurred in the third base dugout area.

"Hey Marcus," Juan questioned.

"Yeah Juan?" I responded.

"What kind of evil entity do you think is in this stadium?" Juan asked.

"You know Juan," I continued, "It's either that murdering husband who killed his wife and her lover, or its something even more evil, holding innocent spirits hostage for its own games."

I came to an abrupt stop, just short of the first row of bleachers down the right field line.

"Did you see that Juan?" I asked. "Out there in center field. It was a blurry, transparent kind of movement, about 30 feet out from the center field fence."

Juan strained to see for himself, leaning over the guardrail, his eyes trained on the center field fence.

"No, nothing," Juan said.

"It was like a blurry entity, that made the advertisements on the left field fence become fuzzy as it moved through the grass," I explained. "I've never seen that before. C'mon, let's get on the field and move that direction."

We climbed onto the right field grass and proceeded to walk toward the center field wall, walking ever so slowly, our eyes focused on the advertisements.

"I don't see anything Marcus," Juan whispered.

"Me either, I agreed. "Let's walk toward the door in the centerfield wall. You know, the one where the scorekeeper came out in-between innings to change the score during ball games."

We walked ahead, slowly scanning in all directions, but focused on the door, about 25 feet in front of us.

"I feel funny Marcus," Juan blurted out.

"In what way Juan?" I asked.

"LIke something is watching us, like it's going to grab us, or something," Juan said. "I feel like we're in immediate dang....AHH!"

I immediately turned around to where Juan was just standing. He was flat on his back, stunned, and unable to speak for a second.

"Juan, what the Hell happened?" I asked loudly.

"Something just knocked me over," he said. "It felt like someone lowered their shoulder and ran at me as fast as they could."

I frantically looked around for the culprit, but saw nothing. Juan began to scream out again as something appeared to be grabbing his foot. His shoe fell off in the struggle, and then Juan's body began to move through the grass, toward the grandstand, while he kicked hopelessly into the air from his back.

"MARCUS! HELP!" he yelled.

The entity began dragging his body faster and faster toward the infield. I ran after him, but could not catch up. The entity was too fast. It appeared to have Juan by his left foot, dragging him toward the third base dugout. Juan was screaming at it, kicking and punching fruitlessly into thin air.

"Hang on Juan!" I yelled out.

I ran as fast as I could, but could do nothing but watch, as Juan was being dragged. Only seconds later, I arrived at the third base dugout and began to frantically look for him, calling his name numerous times. I looked both inside and outside the dugout, but saw nothing.

"Juan! Juan!" I yelled out.

Veronica and Dez came running out from under the grandstand.

"What's going on?" Veronica screamed.

"He's gone! Oh my God, Juan's gone!" I yelled.

"What do you mean he's gone?" Dez asked.

"Something grabbed him and dragged him across the field, and then he just disappeared!" I explained, out of breath.

"What?" Veronica said. "Juan, where are you?"

"Juan!" Dezzy called out.

I was bent over at the waist with my hands on my knees, trying to breathe enough oxygen to catch my breath.

The wind around us began to swirl, quickly picking up all surface dirt around and down the first base line.

"Oh my God, what's happening?" Dezzy yelled out over the increasing winds.

I pointed in the direction of first base and screamed out over the deafening sound of the winds.

"Look! Over there!" I yelled. "Something is manifesting!"

What could be described as a twenty foot high dirt tornado was forming three feet in from the baseline near the pitcher's mound.

"Look!" Veronica screamed out. "Something is in the base of the funnel!"

"It looks like multiple entities!" Dezzy said loudly.

The funnel began to twitch and shake violently. We backed up a few feet and then saw one of the entities thrown from the funnel. It lied motionless on the ground.

"Holy Crap!" I screamed. "It's Juan!"

We ran toward Juan as the dirt tornado moved away and soon disappeared into the outfield grass. I knelt down by Juan expecting the worst.

"Juan, can you hear me!" I asked, tapping on his chest.

"Juan! No!" Dezzy cried.

Veronica kneeled next to Juan and laid her head on his chest.

"This can't be!" she said.

Juan's body was limp.

"He's breathing!" Veronica smiled. "He's alive!"

"And moving!" I said, as Juan's right arm began to move in the dirt.

"What happened!" Juan mumbled.

"Juan, we thought we lost you," I said. "You were dragged by something we couldn't see and then just disappeared into nowhere."

"Yeah, and about two minutes later, you reappeared inside one of those dirt tornados," Dezzy explained. "We saw several entities in there. One was you. Who were the other ones?"

"I don't know," Juan said, pulling himself up to a seated position. "I don't really remember anything."

"Well, whoever that was, they saved your life," I said. "The evil entity, the one that dragged you across the field, was trying to drag you into the third base dugout."

"What the Hell," Juan said.

"Girls, did you find anything under the grandstand by the third base dugout?" I asked.

"Nope. Nothing," Veronica stated. "But we didn't have enough time to check everything out."

Juan stood up, hanging onto my arm for balance. The back of his shirt had numerous grass stains on it and was partially shredded from being dragged through the outfield grass and into the dirt infield. There was some blood seeping slowly through some of the holes on his back. Veronica lifted up the back of his shirt and began to pick some of the pebbles off that had embedded into his skin.

"Dezzy. Do you have that cloth rag with you, you know, the one that you use to wipe off makeup with?" she asked her.

Dez quickly grabbed the cloth and gave it to Veronica.

"Maybe I can get some of this stuff off your back and clean it up a little bit," Veronica said.

"Juan, do you remember anything from the two minutes that you had disappeared?" I asked.

"No man. Nothing," he answered.

"Whatever is in here can zap all of the power that it needs when we are all together, and it can target one of us when we are separated," I added.

"It's a pretty dangerous, and clever, entity," Veronica said.

"What do you want to do next," Juan asked the group.

"Maybe we should knock off for the night," Dez suggested. "You know, because Juan got hurt."

"No way," Juan responded. "Every time something happens, we leave."

"I agree," I said. "This evil entity feels like he can manipulate us each time we come."

"Let's show it what we're made of!" Veronica screamed out toward the grandstand, creating a series of echoes. "We're tougher than you are!"

We sat on the infield grass discussing our next move. A calmness had taken over the entire stadium. It seemed at peace. A very light, and warm wind blew gently into my face from the first base dugout causing me to smile warmly.

"Ah. That wind feels awesome," said Dez.

"Yeah, what a change from 5 minutes ago," I said.

"Hey you guys?" Juan quietly asked.

"Yah Juan?" I answered.

Juan could only point in the direction of the first base dugout. He could not speak any words. His mouth was open and he was as white as a ghost.

I spun around to see what he was pointing at. Coming from the bowels of the stadium locker room area, and through the dugout, was a baseball player. His cream colored, pin striped jersey was clearly sporting the number one on the front.

We sat there on the grass, unable to speak or move. Our bodies were frozen with excitement and fear. His well-toned body and perfectly tailored uniform walked to the top of the dugout stairs, his metal spikes clinking on the concrete. He stopped on the top step. He was slightly blurry, and transparent, a definite ghostly figure.

I reached over to Juan and tapped him on the arm, not letting this apparition out of my sight.

"Juan, is, is that 'The Rocket'?" I asked.

"Yup," is all that Juan could say.

"My God, he looks so young," Veronica said.

"He was only nineteen when he died," said Dez.

'The Rocket' stood there, staring out onto the field, seemingly oblivious to us. It looked like he wanted to run out onto the field, take his position and play just one more time. His eyes seemed sad and his face forlorn, the look of lost opportunity.

We sat there watching intently, waiting for his next move.

"He's turning his head. He's turning our way," said Dez quietly.

We continued to stare until his eyes met ours. I began to shiver up and down my body as his icy glare seemed to pierce right through my soul. His mouth opened and he managed to convey a very simple message.

"Help them.... They are entrapped in this stadium... Release them... Edgar and Joe," 'The Rocket' moaned.

As soon as the message was spoken, 'The Rocket' began to fade quickly, backing down the stairs and disappearing into the dugout. Producing enough energy to manifest is hard enough, but the energy required to manifest, and then speak, is exhausting.

"Wow, just wow!" Veronica said.

"Did anyone have any equipment on to capture that?" Dez asked.

"Oh man. We didn't have anything turned on at all," I said.

"Not even the audio recorder?" Juan asked.

"Nothing," I said.

"That was crazy! And the best experience I've ever had!" Veronica said. "He was so close, spoke so clearly, and had a clear message for us."

"And he was sooo cute!" Dez added.

We stood up, our bodies still shaking with excitement. I high-fived Juan.

"Awesomeness!" Juan blurted out.

"Okay, what we found out today is that 'The Rocket' wants us to help an Edgar and Joe," I said.

"And the murder and suicide are not related to this," Dezzy added.

"Neither is the unfortunate incident with Cody 'The Hammer' Johnson," Veronica said.

"One big question remains, who were Edgar and Joe, and if they didn't die here in the stadium, why are they here now?" Juan surmised.

"Good question Juan," I said.

"Let's do some more searching at the library tomorrow," Veronica suggested. "We need to find out who Edgar and Joe are, and what their relationship to the stadium is."

"And why 'The Rocket' needs to help them," said Dez.

"Lots of questions. We need answers," I added.

We left for home to recharge the batteries, and get some rest. Tomorrow will be another big day.

Chapter 9

ON THE RIGHT TRACK

I awoke the next morning, feeling uncharacteristically recharged and refreshed. My motivation was inspired by what we encountered at the stadium the day before and by our perceived closeness to solving this perplexing mystery.

I hurried to the bathroom to get ready for the day when I heard my mom call up the stairs.

"Marcus!" my mom yelled.

"Yeah Mom?" I shot back while putting the final touches on my shaved face.

"You want some breakfast, Honey?" she asked.

"Naw," I yelled. "I'm heading over to the library for a while this morning. I'll grab some lunch when I get back."

"Alright," she responded.

I usually never missed a great breakfast, but my adrenaline was running so fast, I just couldn't stop my momentum and take the time to eat.

I threw on my clothes and a jacket, and within a few minutes, I began the short four block walk to the Spider Lake Library. Our Para Troupers group was meeting at nine o'clock to do some extensive research of the old ballpark. I figured that, with all of us looking, we should be able to come up with some new leads on who Edgar and Joe are and what their relationship to the Woodticks Stadium is.

I arrived at the library as one of the librarians was opening the front doors.

"Well, good morning young man," the librarian said, as I shot through the door moving quickly toward the microfiche area.

"Good morning Ma'am," I responded while glancing back.

I proceeded to the back of the library quickly grabbing a microfiche reader. I began to research, again focusing on 1931 and 1932.

Juan, Dez and Veronica came soon after, grabbing the other microfiche reader and two computers.

Juan and I focused on 1931 and Dez and Veronica began looking at 1932.

"You know guys, Juan and I already researched the ballpark deaths for those two years. Maybe we should concentrate on other deaths that happened in Spider Lake in that same time span?" I said.

"Maybe Dezzy and I could look at how other Woodtick ballplayers from that era had died," Veronica said. "Maybe they are attached to the stadium or attached to something inside of it?"

"Great idea," I said.

"Marcus and I can concentrate on other death's in Spider Lake during 1931 and 1932," Juan said.

"Yeah," I agreed. "Maybe the deaths happened away from the stadium, but are somehow connected to it."

"Awesome," said Dez. "Let's get going."

We sat there with the screens in front of our faces for what seemed like hours. Most of the deaths during that time were elderly citizens that had passed away from old age, or residents that had tragically died from car and farm accidents.

"Hmmm," I moaned. "Nothing seems to fit the narrative that we're looking for."

"Wait, take a look at this Marcus," Juan read. "It's not confirmed deaths, but it may fit what we're looking for."

I looked into Juan's microfiche reader.

"Hmmm," I said. "The headline in the May 12th, 1931 paper reads 'Batboys Go Missing- Town Stunned'," I read.

Veronica and Dez came running over from their computers.

"What else does it say?" Dez asked impatiently.

I read on. "Two of the Woodticks batboys were reported missing after the game on Tuesday night when they didn't show up at their meeting spot with their parents."

"Did they ever show up? Were they found?" Veronica asked.

"Not sure," I said, "but it happened a couple of days before Cody "The Hammer" Johnson killed Jennifer Stone with that line-drive foul ball in the third base grandstand."

"Wow, how awful," Dez said.

"Let's check the next several days of newspapers and see what happened," Veronica said.

"What were the boys names Marcus?" Juan asked.

I read for another 20 seconds or so before quickly taking my eyes off the microfiche reader and sitting down on the chair. I took a deep breath and sighed.

"What is it Marcus?" Veronica asked. "What are their names?"

"Edgar and Joe Donskey," I said, looking around at my friends sitting in a circle around me.

"WHAT?!" Juan screamed.

"Are you kidding me?" Veronica said loudly.

"Donskey is your mom's bosses last name," Dez said.

"Exactly." I responded. "He was named after his two uncles, Edgar and Joe Donskey, the two batboys that went missing in 1931," I explained.

"This is nuts!" Juan said.

"Okay, why would the ghosts of Edgar and Joe Donskey be at the Woodticks Stadium?" Dezzy asked. "Did they ever find them?" Are they still alive?"

We looked over hundreds of documents and articles over the next few hours looking for answers to those questions. We came up with a few conclusions.

"Okay, first of all, the boys were never found," I explained. "After thousands of man hours looking for them, the searches had turned up no trace of the two."

"Yeah, the search turned from a kidnapping and search and rescue, to a recovery effort, looking for bodies," Juan said.

"How awful," Veronica said. "Those poor parents. I can't imagine the pain they felt all those years, never knowing what happened to their two little boys. I would have lived the rest of my life with a broken heart."

"I'm just sickened by this," Dez remarked.

"Okay, let's try and think through this," I reasoned. "The two lost boys were never found. They worked for the Woodticks team as batboys. That would explain why Johnny "The Rocket" Espinosa was trying to help them. He knew them, and knows that they were never found."

"Yeah, and maybe he's trying to reunite them with their parents who had died years later," Veronica surmised.

"Maybe the evil entity at the stadium is responsible for holding the souls of the lost boys?" Dezzy added.

"Brilliant Dezzy!" I said. "Maybe the person who kidnapped them is the evil entity at the stadium."

"I like it guys," Juan said. "I think we have found a solid direction for this investigation."

"I think 'The Rocket' knows where the boys are," Veronica said. "He knows there is pure evil keeping these boys souls at the stadium. But I do have one question, where are the boys bodies?"

"Maybe that's what 'The Rocket' needs our help with?" Dez suggested. "Do you really think 'The Rocket' knows where their bodies are Veronica?"

"I'm pretty sure he does Dezzy," Veronica added. We need to do more investigating to get more answers. We need to speak with Johnny 'The Rocket' Espinosa."

"Okay, hear me out on this," I said. "It is possible that their souls are still attached to their bodies, and not just attached to some object like the stadium, right?"

Everyone nodded in agreement.

"If that's the case, that means that their bodies could be in the stadium," I added.

"The only problem with that theory Marcus, is that the stadium is older than the boys were when they were taken," Juan said. "Where would someone have buried the bodies? It certainly wouldn't have been in the field somewhere. Someone would have seen the moved dirt."

"You're right Juan," Veronica said. "And everything in, and under, the grandstand is solid concrete and was built more than 100 years years ago."

"Is there any part of the stadium that is newer?" I asked. "Maybe a parking lot, a scoreboard, anything?"

"No man," Juan said. "It's all original stuff."

"Except for the area, in the grandstand by third base, where they replaced the concrete because of the blood splatters from Jennifer Stone," I said.

"You're right Marcus," said Veronica. "Much of the paranormal action happens near that third base dugout. Is it possible that their bodies were buried in the concrete? After all it was replaced just a week or two after the boys were kidnapped."

"Wow, I like where this is going!" said Juan.

"But, and it's a big but, how could the boys be buried in that concrete and have absolutely no one else be a witness to the crime?" asked Dez.

"Great question Dezzy!" I said. "We need to see who the concrete contractor was for the job and find out which of their workers worked on that project."

"One problem, everyone that worked on the job is long gone by now," Veronica said.

"True, but maybe we can find out in the company's records who worked that job, to see who the kidnapper may have been," I said.

"This seems like a solid lead for us," said Dez. "But, not only do we need to find the name of the contractor, we must be able to search the company's records as well for individual employees names."

"Where do we begin?" Juan asked.

"I think we should start by talking with the owners of the Woodticks team," I suggested. "I'm sure they have records of all the contractors over the years that have done work for them."

"Great idea Marcus!" Veronica said.

"Let's start at the Woodticks headquarters at the new stadium," I directed. "They should have all the records that we need to see."

We all agreed to meet the next morning at the new stadium, hoping to find even the smallest bit of information that could lead us to a conclusion.

"The family of those poor batboys have suffered for about ninety years, Veronica said. "It's about time they found peace."

The next morning I awoke to sunshine streaking through my bedroom window. The beautiful songs of a nearby family of cardinals were sending their sweet music through my open window and the smell of fresh cut grass was wafting through the normally stale air in my room.

I laid in bed, eyes closed, enjoying this summery alarm clock, feeling invigorated with our investigation's new direction.

This wasn't going to be easy. I knew that we may encounter a lot of resistance from family, the ball team or others. Contractor, and team records, may be too old to read or simply not available anymore.

My phone began to 'ding'.

Hmmm, text messages, I thought.

I grabbed my phone off the nightstand and pulled it up slowly to my opening eyes. It was Veronica.

'G'morning Marcus', the text read.

'Morning V', I responded.

'Wanna come over for breakfast? Juan will pick us up here at ten o'clock', she text.

'Sure V, see ya in a few', I replied.

I slowly stood up and headed to the bathroom to shower.

It was going to be a big day today, I thought.

I showered, dressed and headed downstairs. Despite the enormously important happenings of the day, I felt sluggish. The adrenaline hadn't been released into my bloodstream just yet. I arrived in the kitchen where my mom was reading the morning news on her laptop.

"Hey Mom," I said. "Have you got some coffee done this morning? I need a little caffeine."

My mom just laughed.

"Are you kidding me Marcus?" she asked. "You've tried coffee a few times. You hate it!"

She laughed again and then pointed to the counter where she had brewed some fresh coffee.

I poured myself a cup of coffee and then went to the refrigerator to get some heavy cream, grabbing the sugar along the way. I dumped a bunch of cream and two teaspoons of sugar into my coffee and stirred it briskly.

"You want some coffee in there with your creamer Marcus?" my mom joked.

I sat down at the table across from her and took a sip. My face scrunched up at the taste of what was in my cup. I cringed at the thought of having another drink.

"You know, this coffee stuff never gets any better," I said.

"You'll get used to it Marcus," she explained. "I was the same way when I was your age. So, tell me, how is it going with your investigation?"

"Well, we are going to the Woodtick offices today to find out who did some repairs at the old stadium. We also found out that Edgar and Joe, the names that keep coming up in my dreams, were the names of two batboys that were kidnapped back in 1931," I said.

"Of course, my mom responded. "I don't think they ever found them, if I remember right."

"They didn't," I said. "Did you know that their last name was Donskey?"

"I did not know that Marcus," my mom said, looking ahead but not making the connection yet.

"That's why Mr. Donskey was named Edgar Joe, after the two lost batboys, his uncles," I explained.

"What? I never would have guessed that connection," my mom said. "Those poor boys... and those poor parents."

She sat there, absorbing the information, before delivering a typical mom response.

"Wow, you guys have certainly become great detectives," she smiled.

"Thanks Mom," I said.

"I'll have to talk to your father about this when he gets up," she said, shaking her head. "He will be very interested to see the information you've uncovered and how this case has turned. Just be careful with this investigation Marcus. I don't want any more reports of injuries, or worse."

"We will Mom," I reassured her.

"Oh, and Marcus," she said, grabbing my arm. "Great job! This family will be so thankful for these answers."

I smiled, took a couple of more sips of my coffee and then left for Veronica's, looking forward to the day ahead.

Chapter 10

MAKING CONNECTIONS

Veronica stood on the front porch waiting for my arrival for breakfast. She was wearing her favorite Woodticks baseball t-shirt and a pair of khaki shorts. Her beautiful, long, blonde hair was up in a ponytail, held together with a Woodticks scrunchie.

She saw me coming down the public sidewalk, stood up and ran to meet me part way down the block.

"Marcus!" she yelled out, hugging me as we met.

""Hi V," I laughed, hugging and twirling her, her feet several inches off the ground.

I spun her around a couple of times and then put her back down on the sidewalk. We began to walk, with one arm around each other, back to her house. We were so comfortable around each other, greetings like this were common between us.

"I am so excited to talk with the Woodticks management today," Veronica said. "I think that we'll get some valuable information."

"Me too V," I responded. "Once we find out the contractors name, we'll go to the contractor and find out who worked on that repair job at the stadium back in 1931, if they still have that info."

We walked into Veronica's house and sat at the kitchen table. Veronica's mom, Lilly, and her great-grandmother, Cynthia, were making breakfast for the family. Veronica's younger sister, Rachel, walked into the kitchen to join us, sitting by Veronica.

"Hi Marcus," Rachel said, looking annoyed.

"Hi Rachel," I responded, smiling her way.

My sister Courtney, and Rachel, were joined at the hip. They rarely spent a day apart from each other, and both had the same irritating whine in their voice.

"Good morning Marcus," Lilly said, looking in my direction. "I'd like you to meet my grandmother," she said, pointing her direction. "Marcus, this is Cynthia. Grandma, this is Marcus, Veronica's, um, friend."

Veronica squirmed slightly in her chair, a little uncomfortable with her mom's introduction.

I reached out and shook her hand.

"What a nice, firm handshake you've got there young man," Cynthia said. "I like that. My husband, years ago, always said that you can trust a man with a good, strong handshake."

"Is your husband here today Ma'am?" I asked.

"Oh no," Cynthia chuckled. "I'm a hundred and two years old. He left me many years ago. As a matter of fact, ten years after he had gone, I married another fine gentleman, and we were together for over sixty years before he passed. He was the love of my life."

"I'm happy that you had that sixty years together," I said. "But, if you don't mind me asking, you mentioned that your first husband left you years ago, did he go off to war or something?"

"Well, I was quite young at the time, seventeen, to be exact," she said. "He was several years older and more experienced than I was. It was bound to be a failed marriage. We were so different. And to be honest with you, he was a little weird, when I think back. Disappearing for several days at a time was a common trait he possessed. He never explained his absences to me, getting downright hostile if I pressed for more information.

After a year of marriage, he woke up and went to work as he usually did, but he never came back. I was crushed at the time, but I never saw him again."

"Wow, sorry about that," I said.

"If I would've stayed married to him, you all would've had a different last name," she said. "As a matter of fact, you'd all be very different people. It's funny how things work out for the better."

"What was his last name, if you don't mind me asking?" I said.

"Donskey," she answered.

I immediately turned to Veronica, my eyes as wide as frisbees. Veronica slowly turned her head toward me and was completely speechless.

"You okay Marcus?" Lilly asked, obviously concerned with the look on my face.

"Um, yeah Ma'am," I responded.

I looked back at Cynthia and asked her one more question.

"Ma'am, is this the same Donskey family that has been in construction here in Spider Lake for generations?"

"Why yes it is," she answered. "My husband, John, started the company, back in 1930, fresh out of high school. We married in 1935. By 1936, he had left me and disappeared. That's when his last remaining brother, James, took over the company. He's the one that really made the company what it is today."

"When did James die?" I asked.

"A little over twenty years ago now," she said. "He handed the company to his son, Edgar, who still runs it today. Edgar Joe. Bless his heart. Good man."

"You mentioned that your ex-husband was the last remaining brother. Was there more than James and John, your ex-husband?" I asked. "What happened to the other brother, or brothers?"

"Tragic story there," she began. "I believe it was 1931. His younger twin brothers, Edgar and Joe, were batboys for the Woodtick team. After a game that summer, they disappeared off the face of the Earth, never to be seen again. Maybe that's why John always acted so weird, and disappeared so often. He was dealing with the loss of his brothers."

Veronica stood up by the table, looking sick.

"Are you okay Veronica?" Lilly asked.

"Yeah Mom," she responded. "I think I need some air. Marcus, you wanna go outside for a little bit with me?"

"Sure," I said. "It was a pleasure meeting you Ma'am," I said shaking Cynthia's hand.

I grabbed Veronica's hand and headed outside. We sat on the bottom step in front of Veronica's house.

"Marcus, I was almost a Donskey," said Veronica. "My great grandma was a Donskey for over a year. She knew Edgar and Joe, the boys that disappeared."

"I know. This is crazy V," I countered. "Let's think about this a minute. You're great grandma was related, for a while at least, to the Donskey family who owns the construction company in town."

"Right," said Veronica.

"That Donskey family has certainly dealt with a lot over the years," I said. "One brother who disappeared forever, two other brothers who had disappeared several years before, and a business that almost went belly up before their big brother stepped in and took over."

"My poor great grandma," Veronica sadly said. "And poor James, who took over the company after losing three brothers."

"He certainly made the rest of the Donskey family proud. He turned that small little construction company into one of the most successful companies to ever take up roots in Spider Lake," I said.

We sat there for a couple of awkward moments pondering the history of the Donskey family.

"Hey Marcus, it's getting late," Veronica stated. "Let's get going to the Woodtick offices and try to find out more information on that contractor that did the cement work at the stadium."

"Yeah, let's get moving," I said.

Veronica went back inside her house and told her mom where we were going. I waited outside until she returned to the front porch. I grabbed her hand firmly and we started to walk to the new Woodticks stadium.

"Marcus?" Veronica asked.

"Yeah?" I responded.

"Do you ever think that if just one of your relatives had married a different person somewhere back in time, that you might not exist today?" she asked.

"Actually, I do think of that quite often," I answered. "Everything had to happen just the way it did, going back thousands of years, for you to exist as you do today. Any skewing of that timeline, might have resulted in a different you."

"EXACTLY!" Veronica said loudly. "I've been pondering this for a long time. Just think, if my great-grandma had stayed married to John Donskey, my mom would have never existed, meaning I wouldn't either."

"It's a good thing that we are living in this timeline, or I wouldn't have you in my life," I blurted out.

I immediately caught myself saying something that I didn't think I was ready to admit. I blushed, looking as red as an apple from Ms. Ardene Miller's house.

Veronica turned to me, and without saying a single word, gently leaned up and planted a soft kiss directly on my quivering lips.

I just stood there surprised, and excited, with Veronica's assertive move toward me. I leaned forward and returned a gentle kiss on her waiting lips. Veronica gently responded by holding my lip between her lips and smiling.

I leaned back to bring her eyes into focus and then gently cleared my throat before whispering a few words.

"I have wanted to do that for a long time V," I stuttered.

"Me too," said Veronica, looking deeply into my eyes. "Maybe we could continue this later?" she asked.

"Um...yeah, for sure," I said nervously.

Veronica smiled.

We walked the last two blocks to the stadium and found Dezzy and Juan already waiting for us, sitting on the bike racks near the front entrance to the stadium.

"Hi you two!," yelled out Juan.

"You ready for this?" asked Dez.

Veronica looked into my eyes, smiled and answered Dezzy.

"I'm ready, if you are," she said.

I was sure that there was a double meaning in how Veronica answered Dezzy's question, so I just went with it.

"Me too," I clumsily blurted out.

Dezzy and Juan stood there, mouths open and eyes wide, just staring at the obvious chemistry between Veronica and I.

"Ah, yeah," Juan said. "I'm not sure what we're talking about here, but let's get going."

We all laughed and then walked up the short flight of stairs and into the door that said '*Woodticks- Front Office*'.

I approached the receptionist sitting at the large, wooden front counter.

"Hi Ma'am. My name is Marcus. We would like to speak to someone about the history of the old Woodticks stadium."

"What type of information are you looking for," the receptionist asked.

"Specifically, we are looking at contractors that the Woodticks organization have used over the past 100 years," I explained.

"Contractors that were used in 1931 specifically, Ma'am," Juan said.

"Our assistant general manager could probably help you out with that kids," the receptionist answered. "His office is through the Woodticks Hall of Fame, down the far hallway, third door on the left."

"Thank you Ma'am," we said.

We entered the Woodticks Hall of Fame.

"Oh my God! You guys! Look at this!" Dezzy exclaimed.

"Wow," was all Juan could say.

Right in front of us was a bust of the late, great Johnny 'The Rocket' Espinosa. On the stand under his likeness, was all of his career statistics with the team.

"Wow, I would've loved to see him play," I said.

"Yeah, he was a very special player," Veronica agreed.

We stood there, for what seemed like hours, just looking at him and his stats, realizing what could have been for this great player. He was certainly the pride of the Woodticks team, and of all of Spider Lake.

"Guys, over here," shouted Juan. "It's a whole section devoted to Cody 'The Hammer' Johnson."

We all raced over to the area.

"Look at this," said Veronica. "He was on his way to the major leagues for sure. He was voted the number one prospect in all of minor league baseball in 1931."

"What a promising future he had," I said.

"Yeah, until he drove that line drive off the head of Jennifer Stone, killing her," Juan said.

"It says here that he was never the same after the incident," I read. "Two years later, he was out of baseball forever."

"Wow, how sad." Veronica said.

"Hey, over here they have a whole display about the twin batboys, Edgar and Joe Donskey," Dezzy said.

We raced over to Dezzy's side and began to read about the boys.

"It says that they had just finished a game, walked down the tunnel toward the locker rooms and then just disappeared, never to be seen again," Juan read.

"Cute boys too," Veronica said. "The parents must've been suffering for years, beyond imaginable. My heart hurts right now for them."

"Me too," said Dez.

Just then, a few footsteps could be heard approaching. A tall, slender man stopped at the edge of the Hall of Fame. He was dressed in a perfectly tailored suit, shiny, black shoes and didn't look very happy to see us.

"Uh, hi there sir," I said.

"Hey, what can I do for you kids?" he sternly spoke.

"Um, we are looking to see which contractor did work in the old Woodticks Stadium back in 1931," Veronica said.

"Why would you possibly care who did work for us ninety years ago?" he asked sarcastically.

"Well, we are doing an investigation that could help solve the missing batboy case from 1931," Dezzy said.

"Really? And you expect to do this now? Sounds like a waste of time to me," the man said.

"No, it's not a waste of time sir," I said. We have good leads that we are checking out."

"The FBI was on the case for years and found nothing," the man said.

"Yeah, but the FBI didn't have the knowledge of the paranormal to help us from the other side," Juan said.

"The paranormal?" the man asked. "You're that group of kids that solved the Rutledge case last year, right?"

"Yeah we are," I said proudly.

"Well, guess what, we don't believe in that hocus pocus crap around here," the man continued. "I have better things to do with my day. See yourselves out please."

The man walked away, back to his office.

"Wow, he was rude!" said Dezzy.

"He's a real f..." began Juan.

"Hey," I interrupted. "We knew that we would get some pushback from some people. It's okay. Let's go."

We turned and walked out, heading for the door. As we walked by the receptionist's desk, we heard a soft whisper.

"Hey kids," we heard.

It was the receptionist.

"I heard your whole conversation. While you were talking with 'Mr. Nice', I did a little research for you. All construction work, including repairs, that we did from 1930 to 1942 was done by only one construction company, Donskey Construction. I hope this helps."

We looked at each other, trying to find words to say.

"It looks like the Woodticks had to start using another construction company in 1942 because the Donskey's were contracted out with the United States military to make tanks for World War Two," the receptionist added.

"Awesome," I exclaimed. "I can't tell you how much this will help us with our investigation. Thank you so much!"

She smiled back at us.

"Thanks Ma'am," Dezzy said as we slipped out of the front door, stopping near the bike racks to regroup.

"Wow, just wow," Juan said.

"So, Donskeys Construction did the cement work on the third base side where we think the bodies of two Donskey kids are buried?" Dezzy surmised.

"This is just incredible," Veronica said. "Is it possible that a Donskey killed the two boys and buried their own relatives in the cement at the stadium?"

"SICK!" yelled out Juan.

"Hey, wait a minute here," I said. "Before we jump to conclusions, we don't even know that there are two bodies buried in the cement at the stadium. We have no idea that the boys were even killed. Remember, no bodies were ever found. We can't be racing to irrational conclusions without any proof, of anything!"

"Marcus is right," said Dezzy. "Let's go right to the Donskey Construction company and see if there is any record of the people that worked on the cement at the stadium."

"Great idea Dezzy," I said. "Let's go right now. Maybe, just maybe, if we're lucky, the person responsible for filling the cement will be named. Let's go!"

Chapter 11

DIGGING DEEPER

We left the new Woodticks Stadium and headed toward Donskey Construction, determined to find out who worked on that cement project at the old Woodticks Stadium.

Donskey Construction was about a mile down the road from the new stadium, so we chose to walk.

"I can't believe this guys," Veronica said. "I was almost a Donskey."

"If there are bodies there under that cement, they could've been placed there by anyone that worked for Donskey Construction," I explained. "Maybe a Donskey wasn't responsible for the deaths of the two batboys."

"True," said Veronica.

"Hey guys," said Juan. "I hate to be the bearer of bad news, but I think that car, back about one hundred feet, is following us."

Dezzy spun around, pretending to talk to us, keeping an eye on the strange vehicle.

"Oh yeah," she said. "He's definitely on our butts for some reason."

"C'mon, let's turn this corner and see if he follows," said Veronica.

We made a sharp right turn onto Kay Street and kept walking forward. The car followed.

"Okay, that's it!" yelled out Veronica. "I'm going to find out who this stalker is!"

"What are you going to do V?" Dez asked.

Veronica took off, running as fast as she could, heading straight for the mysterious car.

"V! No!" I yelled out.

The driver of the car was so shocked that someone would do this, they just stopped the car, as if stunned by her advance. Veronica reached the passenger side window and proceeded to bang loudly on the tinted glass.

"C'mon, who are you!" Veronica yelled out. "Why are you following us?"

We raced back to Veronica's side.

"Veronica, are you sure that you know what you're doing?" Dezzy asked. "They could be dangerous. They could be mobsters. They could be pediphiles! They could be murderers!"

Veronica did not answer. She was focused on the window. We tried to peer through the dark tinted glass, but to no avail.

The car's engine shut off and the driver's door started to open. We stood on the sidewalk waiting to see who stepped out of the vehicle.

A tall, thin man stepped out onto the street. He was dressed in a perfectly tailored, dark blue suit and a large, black fedora hat and sunglasses.

I recognized him right away.

"You're the FBI guy, right?" I shouted. "You're the man in the suit, from our Rutledge case last year."

"Oh, I remember you!" Juan said. "We never knew your name, but you helped us out a lot. You helped us solve that case."

"What is your name, by the way?" asked Veronica.

"My name is not important," he said. "I remain anonymous in my cases so that my identification is kept secret. If criminals knew my name, I'd be hunted down by someone eventually. This way, I can freely move around the town with ease."

"Wow, cool!" said Juan. "He's like a spy."

"I guess you could say that Juan," he said. "I have been following your group for a while now. You have amazing investigative qualities. As you may, or may not know, the FBI is in charge of kidnapping investigations when we think the children taken could travel across state lines. We had been working on the batboys kidnapping case for decades. We finally dropped the case, because the FBI didn't want to go the paranormal route as an option. I'm all about using all available resources to solve a crime, ghostly or not."

"Wow, thanks sir," I said.

"I have been impressed with the progress that you've made so far," said the man in the suit. "You've made more progress than the FBI itself, because you're willing to use all available resources. Keep up the good work. I will always be close by to help, if needed."

"Thank you for your help," Veronica said.

"I like your confidence Veronica," he said. "You have no fear."

"That's Veronica alright," I said.

We all laughed.

"Well, have a good day kids," the man in the suit said. "Be careful. I'll be in touch."

He quickly got back into his car and sped away.

"He's such a mysterious guy, isn't he?" Veronica asked.

"It's good to know that he's backing us up," I said. "But it's too bad that the FBI doesn't consider paranormal entities as a credible source."

"Totally agree man," said Juan.

We continued our walk several more blocks until we found ourselves at the doorway to Donskey Construction.

"This is it guys," Dezzy said, pointing to the sign etched on the front door.

We entered and were immediately greeted by the person at the front desk, a man with a radio headset on, with multiple conversations in progress. He held up his finger, looked over at us, and mouthed the words 'hang on a minute.'

We stood there, patiently, until he was able to speak with us.

"Alright, what can I help you with today kids?" he asked.

"We would like to find out who did the cement work on the old Woodticks Stadium on the third base side of the grandstand," I said.

"Are you talking about the area that we dug up and replaced after that woman was killed by a baseball, back in 1931?" he asked.

"Yes," I said.

"Boy, hmmm, we don't have records that far back," he answered.

At that moment, a familiar face came around the corner. It was Edgar Joe Donskey.

"Hey Marcus!" he said to me.

Shocked that he remembered my name after meeting me just once, I responded.

"Hi sir," I said.

"What can I do for you young man?" he asked.

"Well, we wanted to find out who put the cement in the old Woodticks Stadium after that woman was killed by that foul ball back in 1931," I stammered.

"Well, let's see, I do know that we did the work on that project," Edgar Joe admitted. "We don't have any of those records anymore, but I can tell you that we were a very small company at that time with only a few employees. Whatever work was done on that project was supervised by John Donskey."

"Is this the John Donskey that disappeared in 1936, never to be seen again?" Veronica asked.

"They are one and the same," he responded.

Veronica had that sinking feeling in her stomach that I immediately recognized. I stepped in and asked another question.

"Do you remember anything else about that project that might be helpful to us?" I asked. "We are investigating the disappearance of the two Donskey bat boys, Edgar and Joe?"

Unfortunately, I don't," he answered. "That was long before my time. I was named after my two uncles when I was born."

Veronica was pretty silent after she asked her question. I could tell that she was bothered by his answer.

"Thank you sir," we said.

"You're welcome kids," he responded. "And say hi to your mom for me Marcus!"

"Will do Mr. Donskey," I said.

We left the building. Veronica was still uncharacteristically quiet.

"You okay V?" I asked.

Dezzy put her arm around Veronica as we walked.

"What if John Donskey, who was almost my great-grandfather, murdered his twin brothers and buried them in the old Woodticks Stadium?" Veronica questioned. "Oh my God, the shame that will be felt by the family!"

"Hey look," I said. "We still don't have any idea that the two bodies are at the stadium, or even if they are buried anywhere near Spider Lake. Let's keep an open mind about this until we have more '*concrete*' evidence."

"That's bad Marcus," Juan laughed.

"What's bad," I asked.

"*Concrete* evidence?" Juan joked... "Get it?"

We all laughed, even Veronica. It's the kind of icebreaker that we all needed at that point.

"So where does this all lead us?" I asked the group.

"Well," answered Dez. "We love the old stadium right?"

We all answered in the affirmative.

"We know that the ghost of Johnny 'The Rocket' Espinosa inhabits the stadium. We also have figured out that the evil entity that lives there is probably John Donskey. Plus there could be other entities there as well, right?" she asked.

We all nodded.

"We also know that these two batboys were kidnapped from the stadium grounds and never found again," Dez continued. "So what we really need is to prove that the batboy's spirits, and remains, are at the stadium, right?"

"Exactly," Veronica answered.

"It makes sense to me that we go to the old stadium and try to specifically contact the spirits of Edgar and Joe Donskey," surmised Dezzy. "That way we know who, or what, we're dealing with."

"I couldn't agree more Dezzy," Juan said.

"Me too," said Veronica.

"Okay, it's settled then," I said. "Can everyone go tonight to the old stadium?"

Everyone nodded their heads.

"Let's do this then," Veronica yelled out. "Let's do this for the Para Troupers. Let's do this for the Donskey family. Let's do this for the town of Spider Lake!"

We all cheered Veronica's passionate plea. We all put our arms around each other, and continued forward into the unknown.

Chapter 12

ONE SCARY BEAST

This quiet, innocent, little town of Spider Lake had a horrible, unsolved secret. A secret not for the faint of heart. A secret so horrible that it festers in the hearts of all the townspeople to this day. Two little boys, batboys for the local minor league baseball team, were kidnapped at the old Woodticks Stadium and most likely murdered.

For almost a century now, this tragic tale has had a severe, immeasurable impact on local families.

Parents held onto their children closer as a result of that day, over protecting their loved ones from perceived harm. Kids never walked alone in the city any more. Quick trips to the neighborhood park to play, or to ice skate in the winter, ended up being family activities because worried parents were fearful that their kids were going to be kidnapped. Long lines of cars were commonplace at the schools in town with parents dropping their children off at the school rather than making a risky one block walk. Conditions had degraded so far in Spider Lake over the decades that parents were being questioned by local authorities, and other parents, if they let their kids out of their sight, for even a moment.

It was only in high school that parent's felt at ease enough to let their kids out of their sight and put aside the micromanaging of their beloved children.

Conversations around the town frequently brought up the tragedy in every day discussions, even to this day. It is without a doubt that the lives of all Spider Lakers were profoundly affected, and tragically altered by the events of so long ago.

The FBI couldn't solve the mystery at the time, throwing their hands up in deep frustration, after refusing to consider the paranormal as a tool that they could use while fighting crime.

Unlike the FBI, the Para Troupers investigative team was more than willing to use all of their paranormal resources to take a shot at solving the crime of the century. It wasn't because we thought that we had better investigative skills than the FBI, it's because we recognize the role that the paranormal can, and did, play in this tragedy.

Our role, as it was in the Rutledge Case from the previous year, was to solve this crime and rid the town of Spider Lake of all evil entities. This case has a long trail of victims over the years from the entire Donskey family and the Woodticks organization, to the hundreds of Spider Lake citizens affected by this tragedy. We knew that this was going to be the most challenging case we've ever tackled, and we had a lot of work to do.

Our group decided to return to the old ballpark later in the day and pursue the spirit's of Edgar and Joe Donskey, the twin batboys kidnapped so long ago.

Before I was able to go to work on the case, I had a long list of chores to do at home that afternoon. I also knew that I needed to complete all of them in order to gain permission from my parents to explore the ballpark in the evening.

I grabbed the lawn mower, and the gas can, from the garage and set them in the driveway. I grabbed my earbuds, slid them into my ears and turned on my favorite music mix that I had made the previous week. The music made the work less painful to do and seemed to make the day go by faster.

I started the mower and began to cut the grass, singing to the music as I buzzed the grass in the front lawn.

"*Oh yeah, I need you,*" I sang out loud, as I quickly moved across the front lawn.

"*Baby, I want you,*" I continued.

"What the Hell?" I said aloud, turning off the mower.

I stood there, holding my hands up to my ears, straining to hear it again. The music was still blaring through the earbuds, but I could hear talking in the background, making the music sound like garbled mush in my ears. There was a clear voice talking but I couldn't make out what it was saying. I turned the music to 'bass only' blocking out much of the music.

'*Free them. Free them from their captor,*" the voice coming through my earbuds said.

'*What the Hell?*' I repeated, looking around the neighborhood thinking that someone was tapping into my wifi.

"Who is this," I demanded. "Who's saying this? Who is the captor? Are we talking about the Edgar and Joe? Is this Juan? Not funny man."

Our elderly neighbor came out of her house to grab the mail from her mailbox, briefly standing on the front steps. She quickly retreated inside, locking the door, after she saw me yelling at myself on the front lawn.

'*The Rocket,*' was the only reply.

It was Johnny 'The Rocket' Espinosa sending me the message, I thought to myself. *It sounds more and more like its the bat boys that he's referring to.*

I quickly grabbed my phone from my pocket and started a group text to the rest of the Para Troupers.

'*Just got a message from The Rocket through my earbuds. He said free them. Free them from their captor,*' I text.

'*Wow. Sweet!*' text Juan.

'*It sounds like we're on the right track to me!*' text Veronica.

'*Can't wait for tonight guys!*' Dezzy tweeted.

I continued my chores with the music blaring in my ears, waiting for further voice messages. Sadly, no more messages were heard all afternoon. I quickly finished up my chores for the day and began to put everything away. I walked by my dad, who was grilling outside on the patio. I stopped briefly to let him know that I had finished.

"Hey Dad," I said. "I finished my chores."

"I see that," he responded. "And quickly too. You did a great job on the lawn today."

"Now that I finished, is it okay if I go to the stadium again tonight?" I asked.

"Did you take out all of the garbage too, even down the basement?" he asked.

"Oh yeah, I got it all," I answered. "I even washed all the trash cans out."

"Wow, nice job Marcus," he said. "Yeah, that's fine if you go back tonight. Is everything going okay with this investigation?"

"Yeah great," I responded. "I'm hoping that we can wrap it up soon. But, I need to run Dad. I need to shower and get ready."

"Okay Marcus," my dad shouted as I raced into the patio door and up the stairs to my room.

"Geez, that boy is always in such a hurry," my mom laughed, as she came out onto the patio with a freshly made salad in her hands.

"He'll run into something one day and break it, or himself," my dad laughed.

I got ready in no time and raced downstairs and onto the patio for a quick dinner.

Nothing better than burgers hot off the grill, I thought.

I sat down next to my sister, forgetting the manners that my parents had preached to us over the years. I reached and grabbed food from all over the table trying to hurry the process so I could be on my way.

"Um, Honey," my mom said. "Where are your manners young man?"

"Sorry Mom," I answered. "I'm in such a big hurry, I just want to eat and go. Please pass the ketchup Courtney."

My dad smiled his approval.

I downed my food quickly, got excused from the table, and then took my dinnerware to the kitchen, putting everything in the dishwasher. I ran toward the front door.

"Marcus!" my dad yelled from the kitchen.

I looked back as he approached me.

"Be careful Marcus," he said. "There are many things in this world that are unknown to us, and dangerous. Use the utmost care tonight."

"I will Dad," I said.

I raced over to Juans. The rest of the group were meeting us at the stadium tonight. Juan had all of our equipment ready for the evening so we filled our empty pockets with ghost hunting gear and spare batteries and headed for the ballpark.

Juan and I were to meet up with Veronica and Dezzy at the front entrance to the stadium. When we saw them, Veronica raced over to greet us. She jumped in my arms and we embraced. She reached up and gave me a very friendly kiss on the lips.

"Oh, look at you guys," Dezzy said, smiling from ear to ear.

I was not used to public displays of affection and turned a shade of bright red.

Veronica noticed, and decided to embarrass me further.

"Isn't he so cute?" she said, giving me another peck on the cheek.

"I'm not too sure about that cute stuff," Juan spouted out.

We all laughed.

"Alright," I said, trying to stick to the business at hand. "With all the action in the third base side of the grandstand, I think it's a good idea that we all start there."

"But, we can't be too close to each other because the evil entity grows too powerful, draining the energy from all of us at the same time," Dezzy said.

"Right," Veronica said. "Let's stay about 20 feet apart at all times so we can prevent a repeat disaster. Let's document everything we see and hear and try not to get hurt, or anything."

"Sounds good to me," Juan said.

"Let's focus on the missing batboys. If 'The Rocket' or any other entity contacts us, we'll deal with that as it comes."

"Okay, let's go!" I said.

We walked into the lower level of the grand stand behind home plate and slowly moved over to the third base side. We stopped, took out our ghost hunting gear and did a quick check on our equipment.

"Let's make sure everything works," Dezzy directed.

We all tried our equipment. All batteries were charged and all was working perfectly.

"Dezzy, why don't you and Veronica head down that aisle just behind the third base dugout. Juan and I can go down this one, next to the area where Jennifer Stone was killed," I said.

We moved into our locations and began an audio session to hear any ghostly voices in our presence. I took out my recording device and we started asking questions.

"Hi," I began. "My name is Marcus. This is Juan, Veronica and Dezzy. We are here to talk with Edgar and Joe Donskey. Are you here?"

There was no audible response. The recording continued.

"This is Juan. If you can hear my voice, can you give a sign of your presence. Maybe knock on a wooden post, move a seat, or make some kind of a noise?"

Dezzy's eyes enlarged as the EMF meter in her hands started to show multiple colors. The EMF meter measures the amount of electro-magnetic energy around it. It is said that when a ghost is near, it draws more energy from the area to manifest itself, or make itself known.

"Did you see that guys?" Dezzy asked.

"Wow, the colors were all the way over into the red zone," Veronica said. "That means that its a very strong entity."

I continued to ask questions aloud.

"We know that you're here with us right now," I said. "Can you identify yourself?"

I waited several seconds to give the entity a chance to speak, before rewinding the audio tape to the beginning.

"Alright, let's play this back and see if we have any responses," I said.

The EMF meter continued to display flashing red and orange colors. I hit the play button.

'Hi. My name is Marcus. This is Juan, Veronica and Dezzy. We are here to talk with Edgar and Joe Donskey. Are you here?'

We stood by the audio device straining to hear a response. No answer was heard. The tape continued.

'This is Juan. If you can hear my voice, can you give a sign of your presence. Maybe knock on a wooden post, move a seat, or make some kind of a noise?'

Again, no response. The tape continued.

'We know that you're here with us right now. Can you identify yourself?'

This time, there was no doubt that we had contact with someone. The voice captured on our audio recording was loud and clear.

'I am Johnny,' said the voice.

We looked at each other, eyes opened, blood pumping. Dezzy asked another question.

"Johnny, are you trying to help us find Edgar and Joe Donskey," she asked. "Do you know where they are?"

I stopped the recording device after several seconds and went back to Dezzy's recorded question.

'Johnny, are you trying to help us find Edgar and Joe Donskey? Do you know where they are?'

Johnny responded with a few words.

'Buried... Trapped... Souls... John...'

"Is that John Donskey that you are talking about?" Juan asked.

I replayed the segment again. No new response. The stadium went quiet for 15 minutes, as we continued to ask questions.

"Geez, nothing for a while now," I said. "Where did Johnny go?"

"Maybe he has a game to play," Juan quipped.

"Yeah right," Veronica said. "At least he gave us some confirmation with the few words he said."

"Right," I agreed. "The twins are buried, their souls are trapped and John Donskey is responsible is my guess."

"Hey, is anyone else noticing how the wind has picked up slightly and its cooling down a little?" Dezzy asked.

"Yeah it is," Veronica said. "Let's spread out. Remember we can't be too close to each other if an evil entity is near."

The wind began to swirl on the dirt in the infield causing mini tornadoes about 3 feet high moving across the infield. The winds continued to increase.

"Oh my God!," Veronica yelled out. "Look at the old scoreboard on the center field wall."

We looked out over the field. There was a greenish haze over the entire ballpark. The scoreboard lights had turned on!

"What the Hell?" I shouted out over the deafening winds.

I felt a light punch on my arm. It was Veronica trying to get my attention.

"Look Marcus!" she yelled out.

We looked out onto the field. Materializing right before our eyes were two ball teams about to play a game. To our disbelief, nine players from the Plankton Worms minor league team were in their positions on the field. The Woodticks team was in their dugout waiting to bat.

Our mouths were wide open as we stood there about to witness a baseball game being played with the ghosts of former players. Juan shouted out the first thing on his mind.

"My God, a Game of Ghosts! See, Johnny left us because he had a game to play!"

We smiled and sat down. The winds began to subside.

"Look, the stadium lights are on," I said. "There hasn't been electricity in this stadium for decades."

"My God, can you believe this?" asked Veronica.

"I know all the Woodtick players," Juan exclaimed. "I've seen pictures of all of these guys before. There's Wilbur 'The Rat' Finnegan, called the rat because of his pointy nose and the way he ran so low to the ground. And there's Orville 'Big Boy' Ham, the Woodticks first baseman. He was called 'Big Boy' because he was six feet six inches and weighed over three hundred pounds. This is so awesome!"

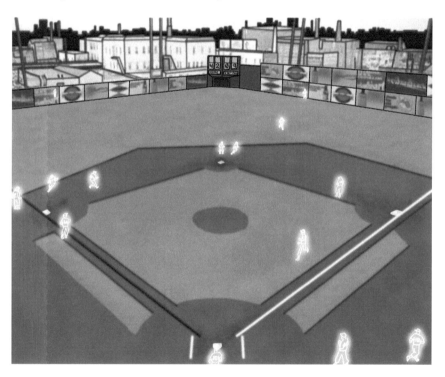

"This must be a residual haunting you guys," I said. "The teams are just replaying the same game again and again, and we are privileged to be here watching."

The public address announcer shouted out the first batters name.

"Up first for the Woodticks, number one, Johnny 'The Rocket' Espinosa."

He slowly walked behind the home plate umpire, stopped, scooped up some dirt from the batter's box area and rubbed his hands together. As he dug his feet into the dirt to ready himself for the first pitch, he slowly turned and looked directly at us.

I felt my heart about to explode with excitement.

"He looked right at us!" Dezzy nervously pointed out.

"This is not a residual haunt, this is interactive," said Veronica.

Johnny was slim. His arms were toned with perfectly sculpted muscles. He looked at ease there waiting for the first pitch, not a care in the world. The first pitch was sent flying into home plate by the Worms pitcher. With one great swing of the wooden piece of lumber in his hands, and a very loud crack of the bat, Johnny made hard contact with the ball.

All the outfielders could do was watch helplessly as the ball sailed far over their heads into the center field stands. Johnny trotted slowly around the bases, enjoying every minute of his tremendous clout.

"Wow," said Juan. "We actually got to witness one of 'The Rockets' many home runs. Man, he had some power."

We clapped as he rounded the bases and stepped on home plate. 'The Rocket' stopped, looked over at us in the stands, and pointed at us, smiling ear to ear.

We sat there, basking in what we just witnessed, when the ground began to shake.

"What is this, an earthquake?" Veronica asked.

"We've never had an earthquake in Spider Lake before," I responded, while hanging on to my seat.

"The players, they're gone!" shouted Dezzy looking over the field. "Quick you guys, spread out away from each other!"

We quickly moved about fifty feet from each other waiting to see what would happen next.

"Hang on guys!" yelled out Veronica.

I quickly noticed that my audio recording device had gone dead, even with fresh batteries. I reached into my pocket, taking some spare batteries out and placed them into the device. They were dead as well.

"Hey V!" I yelled. "How are your batteries?"

"Good!" she yelled back.

"The entity must be by me!" I shouted. "All batteries are dead!"

The ground was shaking violently, the wind was picking up and growing more intense.

A strong gust of wind shot through the grandstand. I struggled to hang on to my seat.

"Help!" yelled Dez. "I can't hang on anymore!"

The strong gust picked up Dezzy, screaming at the top of her lungs, and carried her away into the outfield, about thirty feet off the ground.

"Dezzy!" Veronica yelled. "Hang on!"

I was filled with anger for the entity carrying away my friend. I ran down to the field, yelling at the entity from the ground below.

"Put her down you coward!" I screamed. "Pick on someone your own size, John Donskey!"

The wind stopped instantly. Dezzy was a good twenty to thirty feet off the ground.

"That's right you coward," I yelled. "We know who you are!"

Right at that moment, Dezzy was dropped and sent reeling toward the ground. I moved a few feet to my left in an attempt to stop her fall. Her body came crashing into mine and we both crumpled to the ground. I laid there dazed as Dezzy appeared to be knocked out cold.

Veronica and Juan came running out onto the field, showing no fear of the entity in our presence.

"What are you hiding John Donskey?" Veronica yelled into the sky. "What did you do with those two batboys, your brothers?"

A very evil, low-pitched laugh bellowed from the sky just above us.

"Guys, look over there!" Juan screamed. "Is that, 'The Rocket?"

In the third base dugout was Johnny 'The Rocket' Espinosa. His body was glowing with white light. He was a vision of goodness and strength. He stared out onto the field as if daring the entity to try something.

The evilness that was above us just laughed and then proceeded to lift up Veronica a few feet off the ground.

"Let me go you bastard," she yelled, kicking her legs out.

"Put her down John!" I yelled.

At that moment a white, bright streak of light shot out of the dugout speeding past me on the ground. It was Johnny in full attack mode. This bright light shot into the sky and attacked the evilness surrounding us. Veronica dropped to the Earth.

I ran over to her.

"Are you okay V?" I asked, putting my arms around her.

"Yeah, I'm fine," she said, standing up, attempting to join the scrum before us.

The winds were swirling now. Flashes of white light were mixed with lightning and darkness as the two forces were entwined in a battle of souls.

We backed away several yards as we watched the battle before us.The dark entity began to grow even larger and started to take control of the fight.

In the corner of my eye, I saw a dozen white lights forming in the third base dugout just as the dark entity seemed to be gaining more strength. Then, within a blink of an eye, all the white lights joined the fight.

This was a battle of epic proportions. Lightning and sparks everywhere. Thunderous yells, screams and grunts emanating from the clouds swirling in front of us.

We backed off about twenty feet from the sight before us. The white lights began to take control after a few minutes, encircling the evil blackness.

The earthquake that had rattled us earlier, was beginning again, as a crack in the Earth began to form under the second base area of the field.

We stared in amazement, as black shadowy figures came up from deep inside the Earth, moving quickly across the ground before us. They slithered up into the air, grabbing John Donskey's evil spirit, pulling him toward the crack in the ground. John's spirit yelled, moaned and fought all the way into the Earth.

When the entities were out of sight, the ground moaned and heaved, sewing itself back together. The crack was gone.

The wind had stopped, the feeling of a dark evil force in the stadium was gone. An eery calm came over the ball park.

We looked at the white lights that remained in the air just above center field. Our hearts were racing with excitement. We were unable to speak. One by one, each white light glowed brightly and then shot up into the heavens. When most of the lights had gone, only one remained. It was Johnny.

We slowly walked over to him on the field.

Johnny's bright light was subsiding and a detailed vision of him was beginning to show itself.

"Johnny," I said.

Johnny looked over at me standing there a few feet away.

"Thank you so much for saving us from John Donskey," I said.

Johnny smiled and began to speak.

"I couldn't have gotten rid of that evil spirit without your help kids," Johnny said. "Now that he's gone forever, you can save the spirits of Edgar and Joe Donskey, the batboys."

"We don't know for sure where they are though Johnny," Veronica said.

Johnny moved so gracefully and spoke so fluently. But it was Johnny's time to move on. His soul was being called up to heaven with the rest of his team.

"I needed to free those boys from the evil before I could move on," he said.

His body began to get fuzzy. He was being called.

"Johnny, where are the boys?" I asked.

"You had it right," he explained. "They're free now from their captor, but their bodies must be buried with the dignity that they deserve. Check the cement in the grandstand."

Johnny's likeness was fading in and out. He turned to all of us and tipped his hat, flashing that big smile that he was well known for. His light glowed brightly before shooting into the air and deep into the heavens.

Veronica was overcome with emotion. She sat on the grass and cried. We all did. We were mentally and physically exhausted. Only a few people, if any, had ever experienced what we did in all of human history. We were lucky, and blessed.

After several minutes of regaining our composure, we stood up, looking up into the sky.

"Wow, just wow," I said, wiping the tears from my eyes.

"That was the most incredible thing I've ever seen," said Veronica. "We saw a baseball game between two teams that haven't been around for 90 years, we saw 'The Rocket' hit a home run…"

"…and we witnessed an evil entity dragged down into the ground," Dezzy interrupted.

"And we saw an entire teams souls complete their purpose here on Earth and then shoot up into the stars," I said, with a tear running down my face.

"You okay Juan?" Veronica asked.

Juan sniffled before responding.

"That was the greatest game I ever saw," Juan said.

"Me too Juan," I agreed, putting my arm around his neck.

We decided to gather our equipment and go home. Our mission wasn't over yet. We knew that we'd be back the next day, ready to help the batboys move on as well.

Chapter 13

DETERMINING A MOTIVE

We had learned a lot so far from this investigation. We learned that John Donskey murdered his twin brothers. We found out that Johnny 'The Rocket' Espinosa's soul was stuck here on Earth until he was able to free the twin brother's souls from their captor, and we learned that the boy's physical bodies were most likely buried in the cement in the grandstand.

Even though we had gained all of this knowledge, we still had a few unsolved problems to deal with. How were we going to convince authorities that the boys bodies were buried in the cement at the stadium and that they should look for them there. Why in the world did Edgar and Joe Donskey's older brother murder his younger brothers, and how should we tell the Woodticks organization about 'The Rocket'? He should be properly eulogized and enshrined.

As a part of the paranormal world, we were often ridiculed by non-believers for our beliefs and experiences. Our paranormal track record on this case would be hard for anyone to believe, so we knew that we had an uphill battle going forward.

I awoke late the next morning, eager to tell my parents of our investigation. I threw on some shorts and a t-shirt and ran downstairs for a late breakfast. I raced through the dining room and into the kitchen where my mom was sitting at the table talking with a man, having coffee.

"Oh, hi there," I said.

The man turned around. It was the man in the suit from the FBI. He stood up extending his hand to me.

"What are you doing here sir?" I asked, while shaking his hand.

"Well dear," my mom interrupted. "He heard about lights being on at the old Woodticks Stadium last night and figured that we may be involved. He came over right away this morning."

"It's good to see you Marcus," the man in the suit said, smiling at me. "There is something that I want to share with you."

I sat at the table eager to hear what he had to say.

"I wasn't ever going to share this with anyone," the man in the suit said. "But I feel that now is the time to get this all out in the open."

"Yeah, what is it?" I eagerly asked.

"My last name is Donskey," he said.

My jaw dropped, almost hitting the table. The look on my face would have gone viral if I had a picture of it at that moment.

"My grandfather was John Donskey, the man that disappeared so long ago," he continued.

"Wait a minute," I interrupted. "I thought that Veronica's great grandma, who married John Donskey, never had kids with him before he disappeared."

"They never had kids," he said. "John left town and began a new life in another part of the country, never to be seen here again. That's where my dad was born, and eventually me. I never knew that he had family here in Spider Lake until recently."

"What?" I gasped.

"Your investigation caught my attention because my last name matches the name of the twin batboys that disappeared so long ago," he explained. "I'm assuming that you were at the stadium last night?"

"Yeah we were," I answered.

"Can you tell me what happened?" he asked. "I've told you that the FBI thinks the paranormal is hogwash, but I am a true believer. I think that all avenues should be considered when solving a crime. What can you tell me?"

How was I going to tell him that his grandfather killed his brothers and then skipped town to start a new life? I thought.

I struggled with the words to say.

"It's okay Marcus," he said, putting his hand on my arm in a sign of support. "My grandfather was not a nice guy. We all know that. Nothing you tell me would shock me at this point."

"Well, sir," I began. "We think that your grandfather, John Donskey, um...killed his twin brothers, Edgar and Joe, the batboys."

"Are you sure about this?" he asked. "How do you know this Marcus?"

I proceeded to tell him about our entire investigation, leaving no details unsaid. I told him about 'The Rocket', about the game of ghosts that we watched, about the evil entity, John Donskey his grandfather, holding the boys captive until he was destroyed at the stadium. I told him about everything.

When I finished, he just sat there, his head resting on this clenched fist, deep in thought.

"So sir," I continued. "All we need to do to prove this case, is to dig up that part of the cement in the stadium where we think the bodies are buried. If the bodies are there, we know why, and the case can finally be closed. If the bodies are not there, we'll need to start from scratch, and all of our work was for nothing."

"Thank you so much for all of your, and the Para Troupers, hard work on this case," he said.

He looked at my mom.

"Now, ma'am," he said. "Your company, Donskey Construction, is doing the demolition at the stadium, correct?"

"Yeah we are," she answered.

"Okay, this is what I'll do," he said. "If I can get a judge to issue a ruling to have that area of the stadium carefully exhumed to see if the bodies are there, I will let you know by tomorrow. We'll be able to carefully break up the cement and find the bodies. If a judge won't do it, I will inform you of that too."

"Sounds great sir," my mom responded.

The man in the suit got up from the couch, shook our hands and quietly left the house.

"Wow Marcus," my mom said. "You guys have been busy with this case. If you have solved the disappearance of these poor boys, you guys deserve a commendation medal of some sort."

"Well Mom," I said. "The person that deserves the commendation is Johnny 'The Rocket' Espinosa. Without his constant communication with us, in various ways, we never would've known about the boys, about the haunted stadium or about the Donskey connection. He's the real hero. The biggest question I have is why would John Donskey kill his younger brothers like that? It doesn't make any sense."

"Sometimes killers don't need a motive," she said. "Maybe it was jealousy. Maybe it was all about the control of the Donskey Construction empire. Maybe it was because it was a Tuesday. Who knows what goes through the heads of murderers."

"That's true Mom," I said.

I sighed.

"What's the matter Marcus?" my mom asked. "Why so glum?"

"We just have to find the boys bodies at the stadium," I said. "If they aren't there, it means that they may never be found."

I quietly walked off to my room, deciding to take the afternoon to finish off a homework assignment for Composition class. We had to write an essay about something important to us. I chose paranormal investigations of course. I had a lot to write about.

I worked on the paper all afternoon finishing right before dinner time. I was shutting down my computer when the phone rang. I could hear my mom answering the phone downstairs.

"Hello," she answered.

There was a brief pause on her end of the conversation.

"Oh. Oh, shoot," she continued. "I will tell him right away. Thank you. Hey Marcus, c'mon down right away please!"

I ran down the stairs quickly.

"Yeah Mom. What's up?"

"That was the man from the FBI on the phone," she said. "A judge has refused to sign off on the recovery effort at the stadium. He said that there was no definitive proof, or reason, to declare that area off limits to the wrecking ball. He refused to hear about paranormal proof. And to make matters worse, Donskey Construction begins demolition tomorrow. If they don't have it done within two weeks, they are fined millions of dollars. They are on a tight schedule."

"Oh man'" I said. "We need to figure this out, like now!"

I ran back upstairs and jumped onto my bed, grabbing my phone off the nightstand. I decided to send a group text to the Para Troupers explaining what had happened today so far. Veronica was first to respond.

'Hey Marcus,' she text. 'Wow. Paranormal doesn't really count in law enforcement I guess.'

'Yeah, tell me about it.' I responded.

Juan joined in the conversation.

'What if we go there tonight, get an audio recording of the boys by the cement and give that to the judge for proof?' Juan text.

'Not a bad idea Juan,' I replied. 'The only trouble is that the judge won't believe that's from a ghost. He will say that we just made it up.'

'Yeah, I suppose,' Juan responded.

'Hey, we don't know for sure that they're buried there either,' Dezzy texted. 'We are taking Johnny's word for it. I think we have to have proof for ourselves before we pursue this.'

'Great point Dezzy,' Veronica text. 'We need audio, or visual, proof of their existence at the sight.'

We decided to go back to the stadium later in the evening and get the proof that we needed.

Evening soon arrived and I took off for the stadium again. I had made this trip many times over the last few weeks, but today was the first trip that I wasn't worried about any evil entities that we may encounter. It was a good feeling.

I arrived at the front gates and soon met up with the rest of our group.

"Hey guys," I said. "I am looking forward to this evening."

"Me too Marcus!" yelled out Juan.

"C'mon guys, let's get over the third base grandstand and see what we can find," said Veronica.

We walked into the stadium and walked over to the cemented area where we believed the bodies were buried.

"This is where we will have to make contact," I said. "It's the only place that makes sense."

We began taking our ghost hunting equipment out and made sure all of it was in working order.

"What is that noise?" asked Veronica. "It's driving me crazy. It's like a clicking sound."

"I heard it too," I said. "Look, over there!" I pointed out.

Two men with rolls of wires were at the far end of the grandstand near the top, moving across the seating area. We decided to walk up there and ask them what they were doing.

"Hey," I shouted out as we approached.

The two men responded.

"Hey kids, what's up? What are you doing here? This area is going to be demolished tomorrow morning at 8:00am sharp."

"You mean you're going to blow up the grandstand?" Veronica asked.

"Yup," they said. "It's the quickest way to take her down. We're laying the explosive wires now so it's ready for morning."

"Oh my God," Dezzy said.

We quickly moved back to the other side of the grandstand by third base.

"If they are allowed to blow up the grandstand, the bodies will be lost forever," Dezzy said.

"And there goes our investigation," Juan continued.

"Alright, this is crucial," I said. "Let's start asking questions. Let's get some proof."

We had our equipment out and ready. Juan asked the first question.

"This is Juan," he said. "I am looking for Edgar and Joe Donskey. Are you here with us?"

Our audio recorder was running as Veronica asked the second question.

"Edgar and Joe," she said. "Are your bodies buried right here in the cement where we stand?"

A warm summer breeze began to blow into the stadium as the sun began to fall out of the sky.

"Wow that's a very warm, pleasing wind in my face," I said. "I'm used to strong, cold winds each time I come here. The cold winds of evilness."

We laughed quietly.

"Okay," Juan said. "Let me play back and see if we got any responses."

Juan went back to the beginning and we started our review of the tape.

'This is Juan, I am looking for Edgar and Joe Donskey. Are you here with us?' the tape played.

There was no intelligible answer, but a muffled, garbled whisper could be heard.

'Edgar and Joe, are your bodies buried right here in the cement where we stand?' Veronica's voice could be heard.

'I think so,' was the response barely heard.

"Did you just hear what I did," I asked. "Did a voice say 'I think so?'"

"I heard it too," said Veronica.

"Are Edgar and Joe both here with us?" Dezzy asked.

The paranormal device that can hear ghostly voices and translate them so that we can hear them started to go off as well. It said a one word answer in a computer generated voice.

"Yes," it said.

Juan quickly rewound his audio device and played the same question that was just asked.

'Are Edgar and Joe both here with us?' Dezzy could be heard asking.

'Yes,' was the response on the recorder.

"That is awesome," I said. "We had two pieces of equipment document the voice that we heard."

"They are here!" shouted out Veronica.

"What do we do now?" asked Juan.

"Hang on," I said. "Edgar and Joe, we are trying to help you."

"They have no idea that they were killed so long ago, do they?" asked Veronica.

"I don't think so V," I said. "We must act quickly and respectfully. Edgar and Joe, if you can still hear us, we will be back tomorrow. Promise. And thank you for talking with us."

The voices stopped again for a half hour before we decided to call it a day.

"What should we do now?" asked Juan.

"We have to go see a judge first thing in the morning, that's what we're going to do!" Dezzy said.

"You got that right Dezzy," I responded.

"If we get to the judges house early, we might be able to get that order to halt demolition by 8:00am, the time that the construction crew begins work in the morning.

We decided to meet at my house at six o'clock in the morning and go to the judges house with our new found evidence. It was our last shot at solving this case. The judge needs to believe us. We need to stop the demolition!

Chapter 14

TAKING A STAND

My alarm went off just before five in the morning. I shot out of bed. I was unsure if I had slept at all. I tossed and turned all night thinking about 'The Rocket', about the judge, about the batboys and about the Para Troupers.

It was extremely unusual for me to be the first one up in the morning at our house. I quickly showered and dressed before heading downstairs to meet the rest of the Para Troupers. I grabbed a granola bar and a diet soda from the kitchen and opened the front door.

"I didn't think that you'd ever be ready," said Veronica.

I looked around. Juan Veronica and Dezzy were all sitting on my front porch waiting for me.

"What are you guys doing here so early? Why didn't you just ring the doorbell?" I asked.

"Marcus, we didn't want to wake the whole family," Veronica explained. "That's okay, we were just talking about the whole investigation. We are quite proud of our group and what we have accomplished."

"Me too you guys," I said.

We began the short walk to the judges house talking over our strategy when convincing the judge to issue a hold on the demolition of the old Woodticks Stadium.

"Okay, first of all, the judge is not going to be happy that we are waking him up at this ungodly time of the morning, so he's already going to be teed off at us," Dezzy said.

"I think that this will work, if he only takes the time to listen to us," I explained. "We have the evidence of the boys voices and the entire story. What can it hurt to delay the demolition until the bodies are recovered. It may take just a day."

"That's true Marcus," said Juan. "They have to take the cement down anyway. They need to just take their time in that section of the grandstand and not just blow it up. Although, it would be really cool to see the explosions!"

"Juan," said Veronica. "We don't want to see the stadium blown up either right? We want to save the boys, and save the stadium. Right?"

"Yeah, I know," Juan responded. "I just really like explosions."

We all laughed.

"Okay, there it is," I said. "The judges house."

"Oh, he's going to be so mad, isn't he?" said Dezzy.

"I don't know Dezzy," I said. "I guess we'll find out."

We walked onto the front porch. I pushed the doorbell next to the front door. There was no answer after a minute. I rang the bell again.

The curtain in the window near the front door opened slightly and then closed again. Within a couple of seconds, the front door opened. It was the judge, still in his pajamas and robe. His deep voice crackled a little as he spoke.

"It's a little early to be selling things, isn't it kids?" he asked.

"Well sir," I began. "We have evidence that proves that there are two bodies buried in the cement at the old Woodticks Stadium, and it's set to be blown up in an hour and a half. They just can't do that to these poor boys who have been lost for so long."

The judge looked at each of us. By the panicked looks on our faces, he could tell that we were dead serious.

"You know," he said. "You must have pretty convincing evidence to make me sign an order to pause the work over there."

"I know sir," I said. "Can we present our evidence to you? It will just take a minute."

"Alright, alright," he said. "C'mon in and have a seat over there," he said, pointing to the living room. "You know that FBI guy was over here the other day trying to convince me of the same thing. I heard the whole story from him already. What new evidence have you got?"

Juan pulled out the recording device. We all looked at each other, hoping that this small piece of unverifiable evidence was enough for the judge to change his mind.

"Alright Juan, play what we've got on the tape," I said.

Juan hit the play button and our recorded conversation with Edgar and Joe Donskey began.

'Okay, let me play it back and see if we got any responses.'

'This is Juan, I am looking for Edgar and Joe Donskey. Are you here with us?'

'Edgar and Joe, are your bodies buried right here in the cement where we stand?'

'I think so.'

'Did you just hear what I did. Did a voice say 'I think so?'

'I heard it too.'

'Are Edgar and Joe both here with us?'

'Yes.'

The judge, listening intently, didn't say a word for several seconds as we replayed the recording. After the second replay, he asked a few questions.

"So," the judge said. "You were where in the ballpark when this happened?"

"We were right in the grandstand, on the third base side in the lower section, where we think the bodies are buried," explained Veronica.

"If the boys bodies are here, as you say, this could solve the mystery of the missing batboys that has plagued this community for decades," he said. "Are you ready to handle the media, and social media, attention that this will receive?"

"I don't know sir," I said. "But justice will be served, and that's all that truly matters."

"Hmmm," the judge contemplated. "You know, I will never admit this to anyone else, but I have a ghost that lives in my house too. I think it may be my grandmother."

"You're a believer too, sir?" Dezzy asked.

"I am," he responded. "I can't dispute the evidence before me. I will grant that order, temporarily halting the demolition."

"YES!" Juan shouted.

We all laughed.

"The trouble is, my office doesn't open up until eight o'clock, so the order won't be prepared until around eight thirty," he explained.

"I know," I said. "We can go to the stadium, explain our story to the construction crew and tell them that a judge's order is coming. What have we got to lose?"

"They are under no obligation to halt construction without that order," the judge said. "We may be too late to stop it. I will call the FBI and have them meet me at my office. When the order is done, they will go to the stadium immediately and serve the order."

"Awesome!" I said. "Thank you so much for your help."

"Yes," said Dezzy. "It means so much to us and this community."

We said good-bye to the judge and raced out of the house, running directly to the stadium.

"Can we make it?" Dezzy asked, out of breath from running a few blocks.

"Sure we can," said Veronica. "C'mon, just a few more blocks."

We got to the stadium just 30 minutes before the demolition. We began looking through the demolition workers trying to find the person in charge. Red tape was surrounding the stadium at every entrance, with barricades preventing access to the grandstand. We finally asked a worker who their supervisor was. He pointed out a small trailer home on the property where his supervisor could be found.

We ran to the trailer and burst in. A few workers were standing in the center of the room looking at a blueprint of the stadium, discussing the demolition.

"Um, we're looking for the supervisor," I said. "His name is Charlie."

A very large man, dressed in blue jeans and a checkered flannel shirt, sporting a moustache and a hard hat broke from the group and approached us.

"Yeah, I'm Charlie," he said. "You kids need to leave right away. We're about to blow this stadium apart in a few minutes. Go on, get out of here."

"Sir, Veronica said. "We have a judge's order coming that will halt this demolition until two bodies can be recovered in the grandstand."

"Bodies?" he laughed. "Are you kidding me? We aren't halting anything. If you don't have an order now, you're too late. Now go!" he bellowed, pointing at the door.

"C'mon guys," Veronica said. "I've got an idea."

We left the trailer and walked back to the main stadium entrance.

"We only have about five more minutes until the demolition right?" Veronica asked.

"Right," I said. "And no judge's order yet."

"Don't be mad guys," Veronica said. "Back me on this."

Veronica took off toward the main gate.

"Veronica, wait!" Dezzy yelled out.

"What is she doing?" Juan screamed.

"My God, she's going to halt the construction on her own," I yelled out.

Veronica crawled over the barricades at the entrance, broke through the red tape and ran into the grandstand. Dozens of construction workers ran after her.

Charlie ran out from the trailer, and stopped by us.

"What the Hell is she doing?" he screamed. "She's going to get herself blown up!"

Veronica just bought us some time. We stood there, watching, as the workers raced into the stadium to catch Veronica.

"I'm not going to just stand here while she risks her life," I said.

I ran to another entrance, climbed over the barriers and into the grandstand. Juan and Dezzy followed. Workers were running all over the place trying to corral us so the demolition could continue. I looked around for Veronica. She was nowhere to be found.

I heard Charlie nearby shout out to his crew.

"Damn kids," he said. "Put a hold on the demolition. We'll have to call the police and get them out of here."

That's exactly what we want, I thought. *It's working.*

Within a few minutes, we heard sirens approaching. The workers had rounded us all up and we headed to the main entrance.

"Man, you guys are in trouble," Charlie said. "Trespassing on private land will get you time in jail."

We walked out of the main entrance and toward the police cars. The first squad car opened its door and out stepped a law enforcement officer. It was 'The man in the suit' from the FBI.

He approached Charlie and handed him the judge's order, temporarily halting the demolition of the stadium.

"You sir," the man in the suit explained, "Are directed to halt demolition while we exhume two bodies possibly buried here at the sight."

Charlie looked at the order in his hands, and then handed it back.

"Alright guys," Charlie yelled to his crew. "Shut down for now!"

The coroner's car approached and then parked alongside the squad cars. A man and a woman, dressed in black suits, walked over to our group and said that they were ready.

"We need your equipment to break down the cement," the man in the suit said to Charlie. "It's going to be a tedious process, so care must be taken at all times."

"Rick, Sarah," Charlie yelled out. "Grab your jackhammers and give these people a hand."

We all walked into the stadium and to the area where the new cement was laid down after Jennifer Stone's untimely, and tragic, death. After a couple of dozen seats were removed from the area, the jackhammers began to carefully, and slowly, chop into the cement. Every half hour, a crew of police officers and coroner staff sifted through the debris looking for any signs of human remains.

After several hours of work, the coroner raised his hand and yelled out.

"Whoa whoa!" shouted the coroner.

He carefully lifted a small bone fragment from the rubble before him. Everyone gasped.

"This is a human remain," said the coroner. "It's a leg bone from a child."

Veronica began to cry. It was more of a release of emotion than anything else. This investigation had been very physically and mentally hard on us. We all sat down in nearby seats and watched as the rest of the boys remains were found and carried away in the coroner's vehicle. Even though the bodies were not clearly identified yet, we were confident in knowing that the boys were found today.

Autopsy results that would identify the bodies would not be ready for several days.

We knew who they were. These two poor boys, Edgar and Joe, had been murdered by their evil brother John and their souls held captive for decades. Because of their older brother, they were unable to move on to the afterlife.

We had pretty much decided that finding a motive for this gut wrenching case was going to allude us this time, but the sheer relief and satisfaction that we felt from solving this case, made everything that we did worth every ounce of effort that we gave.

The man in the suit approached us as we sat in the grandstand seats.

"Hey kids," he said. "This community and the Donskey family, owe you a huge debt of gratitude for solving this case. My grandfather was not a good man, he was evil. But you found out the truth. You have saved lives, and many souls, in this case. I am so proud of you and your efforts."

"Thank you sir," we said.

"I hope the boys spirits can move on now," I said. "That's my concern."

"Me too Marcus. Me too," said the man in the suit.

Chapter 15

A PROPER BURIAL

Several days had passed since the bodies were recovered at the old stadium. The autopsy results had been released by the coroners office proving that the two bodies recovered at the scene were, indeed, the two missing batboys.

The evil entity that had lost its grip on the boys souls had moved to the realm of darkness below for its evil deeds. Johnny 'The Rocket' Espinosa and his band of fellow Woodticks teammates had moved on to the after life. One would think that these conclusions would only indicate a job well done. This was not over yet. Serious questions remained.

What was going to happen with the old Woodticks Stadium, and what was to become of the batboys souls. We always saw souls rise into the heavens with a flash of light. Even though we had just communicated with the pair the day before their bodies were found, proving that their souls were still with us, no sign of the boys moving on had been seen.

The Donskey family, after mourning these two long lost souls for so long, were quietly planning a long overdue burial for their two treasured boys.

The townspeople of Spider Lake felt like a weight had been lifted off their backs with the conclusion of our investigation, and after the autopsy results were released.

I, on the other hand, began to prepare for the very public funeral services that were to be held later in the day and for the onslaught of social media attention that we were bound to attract with our latest accomplishment.

I had attended memorial services before with my family a few times in the past, but this one was going to be much different. The national attention that this story will receive was way beyond anything that I have ever experienced. I tried to maintain my focus and attention as I worked through the morning hours at home.

I decided to give Juan a call. I grabbed my cell phone off of my dresser, dialed Juans number and then put the phone on speaker so I could continue to get ready for the funeral services.

"Yeah hello," said Juan.

"Juan," I said. "I cannot figure out how to tie this stupid tie. My dad taught me once a long time ago but I forgot. You ready?"

"Yeah, yeah," said Juan. "Man, I hate getting dressed up. Do you think the Donskeys would mind if I wore my jeans?"

"Yeah, not a good idea Juan," I laughed.

"Hey, what time are you getting to the funeral Marcus?" Juan asked.

"I dunno," I answered. "Maybe 9:45ish?"

"I'll shoot for that as well," Juan said. "Hey, let's meet in front of the Johnson's funeral home and we can all sit together? What do you think Marcus?"

"Sounds great Juan," I said. "Of course, that's if I can get this tie to work for me," I laughed, looping it around my neck.

"Yeah, I like that too," Juan explained. "It shows the unity that we have in our group and the unity that we have with the Donskey family."

"Alright man," I said. "Sounds like we're on the same page Juan, my man. See ya later."

"Later," Juan said.

Our whole family was going to attend the services today. We were all dressed in our finest black clothing as we headed to the car for the ride across town. I had never seen our family so dressed up, looking so proper, before.

I gazed around the car at my family as we drove. I really loved them all, and appreciated each one so much. Maybe my thoughts were being influenced by the paranormal excitement and stress of our investigation. But I thought, just for a moment, how well put together and proud I was of my family.

Our normally chatty family was very quiet and somber as we viewed the beautiful scenery of Spider Lake through the car windows. A feeling of contentment rushed through my body as I sat there, smiling to myself.

We approached the funeral home and found that every parking space was taken within a few blocks of the sight.

"Man, it looks like the whole town is here for this," I said.

"It sure does Marcus," my dad said.

We continued to look for parking finally finding a spot down the street from Johnson's Funeral Home. We parked there and walked a few blocks back to the funeral home.

When we arrived, I found the rest of the Para Troupers standing near the front entrance waiting for me.

"Wow, Veronica and Dezzy, you guys look, well, beautiful," I said.

The girls were wearing their best, and most respectful, black dresses. Their hair curled and styled, small black purses and black pumps on their feet to match.

"Thank you Marcus," Veronica smiled.

"Thanks Marcus," said Dezzy. "I like what you said more than what Juan said."

"Juan, you didn't," I said, looking over at Juan with his head down.

"Yeah," said Dezzy. "All Juan said was 'You girls clean up well'."

"We knew what Juan meant," said Veronica. "It was a compliment. We get it."

The girls put their arms around Juan and gave him a big hug until he smiled. We all laughed.

"C'mon guys, let's find a seat," I said. "It's almost ten o'clock."

We walked into the expansive welcoming area. The room was completely filled with fellow Spider Lakers, old ballplayers and the Donskey relatives that came from all over the country.

Juan leaned over toward me and whispered.

"Marcus, did you look around? Every Donskey in town is here," he said.

"It looks like the whole town is here Juan," I smirked.

We all sat quietly as the service began. In front of the room, sat two identical caskets, about half the size of normal adult one's. Flowers completely surrounded the entire room, sent by people from the community, family members and former professional ball players and friends. Jerseys from the batboys were hung in front and a bat signed by all the current Woodticks players stood next to the caskets. The pastor spoke from a podium at the front of the room.

It was a beautiful service, filled with memories of the boys, pictures of the old Woodticks team and shared stories from so long ago from members of the community. The service lasted almost one and a half hours. Many elderly people from the community eulogized the boys during the service remembering the boys when they attended games as children. It was a very moving experience.

When the service concluded, we got into our vehicles and formed a long line behind the hearse that carried the two batboys and a few members of the Donskey family. We drove along Espinosa Way, right passed the old Woodticks stadium, that held onto the secrets of the past for so long, turned right onto State Highway One, and then right through the cemetery entrance.

Our cars circled around near the area of the gravesite as we exited our vehicles and gathered around near the graves. The caskets of the boys were carefully taken from the hearse and placed next to their graves as the internment began. We stood in utter silence as the pastor gave his impassioned plea to the heavens above to save these poor boys souls.

I glanced around as the pastor spoke. Everyone was either weeping openly or had sad, heavy hearts and tears in their eyes. I lowered my head a little and Veronica leaned over and grabbed my hand. It wasn't the typical nice hand holding that we always did, it was an aggressive 'Hey look at me' kind of grab.

I looked up at Veronica. She smiled and nodded her head toward the batboys caskets. I turned to look and saw a strange, glowing light slowly descending from up above. I quickly looked around at the others in attendance, seeing if we were the only ones noticing this event unfolding in front of us.

This bright orb continued to free fall from above slowing as it approached the two caskets. I could not believe that no one else was witnessing this. I looked at Veronica. She began to tear up, not trying to conceal her emotions.

The orb hovered about three feet over the two boys for just a few seconds before two smaller orbs appeared from the top of the caskets.

I looked over at Juan and Dezzy, both appearing sad and sullen. I looked to my left and smiled at Veronica. She returned the smile, her cheeks were wet with tear drops. She looked as if she was going to burst out crying. I moved over to her and put my arm around her shoulders.

"Are you okay," I whispered to her.

"I think we're the only ones that can see what's happening Marcus," she whispered.

I looked across the gravesite toward the batboys caskets. There was a hazy, green mist surrounding the area. The sunlight peeking through the haze made for a very eerie sight. Hovering above the caskets the three orbs of light began to fade as three figures began to appear. I recognized the largest one immediately. He had the number one on his jersey. I was 'The Rocket' in all of his glory. He appeared to be hovering above the boys caskets with his arms firmly embracing the two batboys, Joe and Edgar Donskey.

'The Rocket', flashing that revered smile of his, looked down at the two boys next to him and then up at us. I was feeling overwhelmed, almost weak in the knees, as 'The Rocket' mouthed two words that we'll never forget.

'*Thank you,*' he said.

The boys looked over at us and smiled as the three entities began to blur, creating three bright orbs that lit up the caskets below.

Veronica was about to bubble over in a very uncharacteristic display of emotions, when in a flash, the orbs shot up into the heavens right before us. We both began to openly weep as we were overcome with what we witnessed. I hugged Veronica tightly until the service concluded.

We had experienced something that very few had ever witnessed. We were allowed to see these visions for some reason unknown to us.

Juan and Dezzy came over to us after the service and we all hugged.

"Did you guys see the entities that showed themselves during the service?" I asked them.

They did not. We took the time to tell them what we had seen, and experienced. This was truly a special day for us, and for the Para Troupers.

We got into our cars and headed to a small luncheon, put on by the Donskey family. Our family chose to drive past the old stadium on the way, getting a last glimpse of the stadium before demolition the next day.

As we approached, we noticed that the large demolition equipment had been moved out from in front of the parking lot. The red tape that surrounded the grandstand had been removed and the barricades no longer blocked the entrance to the stadium itself. We pulled into the lot and parked next to the old bike racks.

We got out of the car and stood there, looking for any clue as to what was going on.

"Mom," I asked. "Why has your company pulled all of their equipment from the site?"

My mom shrugged her shoulders.

"I'm not sure Honey," she answered.

We heard a loud squeaking noise coming from inside the grandstand that sounded like a large metal door opening on its hinges. A man walked out from the entrance and into the parking lot. It was 'The man in the suit' from the FBI.

I walked forward and approached the man.

"Hi sir," I asked. "Do you know what's happened to all of the demolition equipment?"

"Hi Marcus," he said, shaking my hand, waving to the rest of my family standing by the car.

"As you know Marcus, I am a Donskey," he said. "Unfortunately, I am the grandson of the Donskey that carried out this evil act, not only on these two boys, but against the Donskey family and reputation."

I stood there quietly as he proceeded to explain.

"My grandfather made a very good living in his time. It's the Donskey way I guess. We all come from generations of success stories. We always worked hard, saved our money, and passed that work ethic along to our children, and so on. Anyway, he left me a very large amount of money when he passed on," he continued. "I have used that money to buy this stadium property for a very good price from the city of Spider Lake."

"You did?" I asked. "Why? It is nothing but junk now, even though it has a glorious history."

"I decided to buy it, and convert it into a Woodticks Hall of Fame, like a shrine to all of the Woodticks players, coaches, trainers, owners and fans of the past," he said.

"Wow, cool!" I smiled.

"It's the least that I could do to help repair the Donskey name, and to honor the great people of the past," he said. "Construction of this new hall of fame will begin as soon as possible."

"Wow, cool," I repeated. "That is an awesome idea."

"Our first inductee into the Woodtick Hall of Fame will be Johnny 'The Rocket' Espinosa," he said.

"And rightly so," I agreed.

"I've decided that there will be a small section of the complex devoted to the Para Troupers, and the work that you did to solve the mystery of the two missing bat boys."

"What?" I asked. "That is about the best thing that has ever happened to me in my whole life."

The man in the suit laughed.

"Thank you, again, for the Para Troupers work on this case," he said, glancing into the sky. "Somewhere, up there, are some very grateful souls."

I smiled, said goodbye, and walked back to the car.

"I can't wait to tell the Para Troupers about this!"

The End